Perilous Healing

COASTAL HOPE
BOOK FIVE

JESSICA ASHLEY

B.A.D. PUBLISHING CO
believing in the power of reading

PERILOUS HEALING
A Coastal Hope Novel
By Jessica Ashley
Copyright © 2024. All rights reserved.

This book is a work of fiction. Names, characters, places, businesses, and incidents are products of the author's imagination or used fictitiously. Any resemblance to actual persons, living or dead, places, or actual events is entirely coincidental.

No part of this book may be reproduced or transmitted in any form by any means, electronic or mechanical, including photocopying, recording, or by any information storage and retrieval system without written permission of the author, except for use of brief quotations in a book review.

Scripture used in this novel comes from HOLY BIBLE, New International Version®, NIV® Copyright ©1973, 1978, 1984, 2011 by Biblica, Inc.® Used by permission. All rights reserved worldwide.

Edited by HEA Author Services
Proofread by Love Kissed Books
Cover Design by Covers by Christian
Photographer: Wander Book Club
Model: Lucas

Perilous Healing

She broke his heart. But now, this former SEAL is her only hope of surviving what's coming.

Shortly after returning home from being held captive overseas, former Navy SEAL Silas Williamson found himself sole guardian of his four-year-old niece.

Moving to Hope Springs was supposed to be a safe haven for them both, but then *she* showed up. The woman who has haunted every moment of his life since they parted ways a decade ago.

Bianca Theodore has certainly suffered through her fair share of dark times. As a military trauma surgeon, she's saved more lives than she can count. However, there was one life she refused to save. And after years of hiding... those who know she's responsible have found her.

As Bianca faces the nightmares of her past, she turns to Silas, who is haunted by his own. Together they stand a chance at surviving the coming battle, but only if they turn to the One who can bring them the peace they so desperately crave.

If you are looking for a sizzling (but not spicy!) romantic suspense, with a protective hero struggling with his faith, a talented surgeon fighting to survive, a small town that protects their own, and a team of wounded veterans turned private security officers, then Perilous Healing is for you!

This Christian Romantic Suspense deals with:

-Coping with trauma

-Discovering your worth

-Seeking God in everything

-Healing from your past

The Coastal Hope series can be enjoyed in any order!

I grew up knowing who Jesus was and a basic overview of what He did for me. It wasn't until I was sixteen, and went to see Passion of the Christ with some friends, though, that I TRULY began to understand the sacrifices He went through. The pain He suffered so that I might have salvation.

Even still, we weren't a Sunday morning church pew family. I wish we were, truly, I do, but it was never a priority in the home I grew up in.

Over time, I continued to waver in my faith, straying further and further off the path until shortly after my sixteenth birthday, I completely lost my way.

I remember exactly when it happened. The shift in my mind when I went from an innocent teen to a girl chasing love in any form.

With every passing year I got angrier and angrier,

moving further and further from where I was supposed to be.

Then, I joined the Army and the rest of the person I was got lost along the way. I was drinking heavily, partying constantly, and doing my absolute best to ignore the fact that I KNEW everything I was doing was wrong, but that dark voice in my head kept stoking the anger.

Those intrusive thoughts kept driving me further and further into the dark.

And then I broke. There was a point I remember sitting on my couch, being absolutely miserable, hating life, and needing a change. I joined Match.com, did some searching, and set up my first date with someone who was the complete opposite of anyone I'd been dating.

A week later, I met my now husband.

Things started looking up for me then, but I still hadn't completely found my way back.

My husband, who grew up Catholic, took me to a church with him. We didn't go every Sunday, but he got me praying before every meal, and we attended as we could.

I remember the first visit we made down to his parents' house in Houston, and how absolutely wonderful I thought it was that they had a family prayer they said each and every night. A prayer that my husband and I taught to our kids, and still say every single night.

Years went by, we welcomed three beautiful children, had them all baptized in a WONDERFUL church we'd found and still attend, and I kew that God loved me. That even though I am undeserving, Jesus sacrificed his life for me. For all of us.

And even as I knew that, it wasn't until 2022 that I started really feeling a pull in my chest. A warmth that settled in and had me craving more out of my faith. I wanted to know more. Be more. Understand more. Jesus died for me and I wanted to start living for him.

I picked up my Bible.

We started attending church every Sunday, making it a priority in our home.

We began truly looking for God in everything, and praying to Him that the Holy Spirit would continue to grow within us until it was so bright, there would never be a question that we belonged to Him.

Which is what led me to write this series.

The Coastal Hope series, and especially Perilous Healing, is my love letter to everyone out there facing struggles. To those who are actively seeking their faith, and to those who have already found it. To those who are still unsure, and those that have been so blinded by pain that they lost their way.

I promise you that all you have to do is seek God and you will find Him.

He's never far.

And if you're sitting on your couch, alone and miserable, crying and desperately needing something... seek Him.

God is there and He will never turn His face from you.
Psalm 34.

-Jessica

To those seeking peace.

CHAPTER 1

Silas

TEN YEARS AGO

Sweat clings to my damaged body like a second skin. There's not a single part of me that doesn't ache. I can't even feel the still-healing stab wound in my shoulder anymore, thanks to the bitter cold spreading through me.

Has death finally come for me? Has the end to my torment finally arrived?

I think of Sierra. My twin sister. She's who I'll miss the most. But at least she'll never see me as haunted as I surely am now. The screams of my murdered teammates echo through my mind on constant repeat. I wish I could drown them out now. There's a part of me that yearns for the torture River Culvers enjoys sending my way, because at least then my own screams eclipse everything else.

Lately, in the small moments of sleep I catch, I dream of the farm back home. Of my dad out working the cattle and my mother tending to the garden. I dream of running through fields with my sister. Of sitting on a porch swing and drinking sweet iced tea.

Why couldn't I have just been content with that life? Why did I feel this burning desire to find more? Look where it got me. Tortured in a country I probably wouldn't even be able to find on a map.

The door scrapes open somewhere behind me.

Where I used to feel fear at their arrival, now I feel nothing. I've grown numb. What more can they take from me when they've already stolen everything?

"Come back for more?" I sneer, my voice hoarse and unrecognizable.

The new arrival doesn't speak, and when he comes around in front of me, I note that I've never seen him before.

"Who are you?" I demand.

"Someone who is here to help you." He reaches up and undoes the shackle around my right wrist.

I fall, unable to support my own weight. He catches me though, holding me up as if I weigh nothing while he undoes the shackle on my left arm.

The stranger takes my full body weight and guides me over toward the chair River sits in whenever he comes to watch me bleed.

"This is a trick." I try to squirm against the man's hold, but he keeps me upright.

"No," he insists. "But you need to keep your voice down. Let's not make this more complicated than it needs to be." The man pulls back and grips my face. "Look at me, Silas."

They call me SEAL here. Or Williamson. Never Silas.

"Who *are* you?"

"I'm here to help you. Now listen to me. You are going to leave this room and head left down the hall. There are some turns you'll take as the hall veers off, but there's a door at the end that will lead you out of here. It will be unlocked for you. Get out, go right. There's a tunnel under the fence. Use it to get to freedom."

I narrow my gaze on him, feeling a bit of my strength return with each passing moment. "Why are you doing this?"

"Because there is more for you to do in this life," he replies as he pulls me to my feet. "Get out of here. Move fast. Remain quiet."

I nod, still unsure if this man can be trusted. It wouldn't be the first time River has toyed with me like this. Last time, he set his dog after me. What if this is another trick?

Go.

The word echoes through my mind.

"Go, Silas. If you don't, you will die in this place. I will make sure the door is unlocked and the path clear." He smiles softly at me, then slips out of the room.

I stare after him a moment, trying to figure out just how I'm going to get the strength to walk out the door, when mere moments ago I thought death had come to collect me.

Go.

That word again. I stand, putting one foot in front of

the other until I reach the door. Then I slip out into the hall and head down the left side just as the stranger told me to. I don't let my mind wander on worries, I just focus on that one silent order.

Go.

Everything aches, my body burning with each movement. But as I make my way down the damp, concrete hallway, I know that if I stop—even for a moment—it will mean death.

He helped me escape this time, but I know that I'll never escape again.

So even as every movement is yet more torture, I continue pushing forward.

I step on a clump of concrete breaking away from the tunnel floor and pause, hissing through clenched teeth as it bites into the soft flesh of my bare foot. Warm blood trickles from the injury, but I have nothing to wrap it. Even if I did, I can't risk the time it would take to do so.

Soon I'll be pushing through a door and taking my chances in the deep jungles surrounding the area I've been held in since I was captured almost a month ago. But dying out there is a lot more enticing than living in this perpetual hell.

I'll happily take my chances.

Each step that takes me closer to freedom cements my desire to survive. I have to make it home. If not for me, then for my entire team who didn't make it through our initial contact with the American crime boss we were here to stop. My command has to know what happened. They have to know so they can act.

Still, people will say I'm lucky. But to me, luck would have been bleeding out on the ground before they ever brought me back into the compound. Then I wouldn't carry the weight of everything that was done to me over the past three weeks.

A woman's scream rips through the stale air, and I sink against the wall, hiding in the shadows. My heart pounds, my head burning with an ache I'm sure will split me in two if it doesn't stop soon.

"Is that all you've got?" she yells. *American.* Though I'm not surprised. The compound we're in belongs to one of the most notorious drug runners in the U.S. Most of the guards are American, except for the one who let me go.

"You let him die!" a man bellows.

"And I'd do it again!" she retorts, then cries out once more as the resounding crack of a slap echoes down the hall. I clench my hands into fists, then take a deep, steadying breath and wait for it to be safe. I should just leave. Continue sneaking out, but if I do—if I leave this woman behind—what kind of man does that make me?

Save her. The two words come to me clear as day, surely my conscience telling me that I can't leave her here. It's the same stern order as the word *go.* The same push toward action.

Even if I don't know her, I *have* to save her.

Even if it means we both get caught, I *have* to take her with me.

I've never been more sure of anything in my entire life.

A door along the wall opens, and two men stalk out.

"I'm going to go find out what we're supposed to do with her. My guess is they'll want her head for this."

"Shame, it's a pretty head," the other replies.

The door begins to swing closed, so I retrieve the chunk of concrete I stepped on and rush forward to catch the door before it locks shut. Then I wait to make sure the men keep walking. One thing I've learned, arrogance does not equal intelligence. If they're so arrogant to believe they're untouchable here, they won't notice something as simple as a door not closing when it should.

Sure enough, they keep walking, so I sneak inside, prop the door open with the concrete chunk, and turn.

I'm standing in what is clearly a surgical room of some kind. There's a hospital bed streaked with blood and an assortment of medical tools and supplies. The woman is chained to a chair, blue scrubs bloodied. Her dark hair falls like a curtain in front of her face, though her breathing is steady enough to show she's alive. There's a tray of sharp tools to her right, so I reach over and grab a scalpel.

"Come for more?" she demands, then looks up at me. I'm pinned beneath a mossy green gaze, though both eyes are bloodshot. Her face is bruised and bloody, and a large scratch runs down one side of her cheek. "Who are you?"

"Chief Petty Officer Williamson, ma'am," I say as I rush forward and cut through her bindings. "I'm getting out of here, and I'm taking you with me."

"Just like that?" she asks, rubbing her freed wrists.

"Just like that," I reply.

"You don't even know why I'm here."

"I know you're not supposed to be here and that these men are going to kill you."

"And you can't let that happen."

"No ma'am, I can't."

"So you're a Boy Scout, then." She stands.

I study her, trying to decide whether or not I've made a mistake. "No, I'm a SEAL."

"Navy," she replies. "You're all Boy Scouts. I'm Bianca." She looks me up and down. "You look pretty bad yourself."

Glancing down at my blood-streaked bare chest and what's left of my uniform pants, I can't argue with her. I don't even know what my face must look like. It's likely even more battered than hers. "I'm not trying to win any beauty pageants," I tell her. "Now, are we going or not?"

"Let me grab some things." She rushes to the side and grabs a blue bag, then stuffs the supplies from the tray inside. "Ready."

Keeping the scalpel in my hand, I creep toward the door and peer out. The hall is still empty. Remaining in the shadows, I stick close to the wall, trying to pay attention to any sounds that might signal trouble.

There's yelling somewhere, though it's so distant I can't quite make out where it's coming from, but I still pick up my feet faster, moving as quickly as I can through the hall until—I spot the door up ahead.

Freedom.

"Shut everything down!" someone screams from behind us. "We have two escapees!"

I reach back and grab the woman's hand, then yank her forward as I sprint toward the exit. If they go into lockdown, we'll never leave this place. I know it deep down in my soul. So I run.

Even as my feet sting.

My muscles burn.

My head pounds.

I hit the heavy door and shove it open, then close it softly behind us to avoid any loud noises, before we sprint into the trees. It's dark overhead, so watching where we're going is an impossibility. There's yelling from the compound behind us, and it just forces me to run faster, to push my body as hard as I can.

But it's not a maintainable speed, so I can only hope we can outrun them before I lose it. I'm just grateful Bianca is keeping my pace with relative ease.

I'm not sure how long we run, but by the time dawn is breaking, I no longer hear anyone behind us. So, choosing a large tree to take cover against, we stop to rest. My breathing is ragged, my body numb from the chill in the air and likely the amount of blood I've lost over the past few hours since two of my crudely stitched stab wounds have reopened.

"I need to look you over," the woman says as she kneels in front of me and opens the bag of stolen supplies. "Otherwise you're going to die before you can get us out of this place."

"You're a doctor?" I ask.

"Trauma surgeon," she replies. "Bianca Theodore at your service. Though I normally treat Rangers, I think I can make an exception for a SEAL this time around." She flashes me a smile that I know is meant to be disarming as she slips into a pair of gloves she pulled from the bag. "This is not going to feel great," she warns, then gently presses against one of the wounds in my side. I hiss through clenched teeth as pain shoots up through my body. "Yeah. So listen, I know we just met and all, and I hate causing pain to people who just saved me, but you should know—this going to hurt—badly."

CHAPTER 2

Bianca

PRESENT DAY

Body slick with sweat, I take out the frustrations of yet another sleepless night on the heavy bag swinging in front of me. I don't know why I'm surprised. It's not like I've had a solid night of sleep in, well, ever.

A childhood of nightmares blossomed into an adulthood of the same.

Round and round we go. If only I knew how to get off this ride.

"You're here early."

I stop hitting the bag and turn to face Michael Anderson. I've known the man for years, and a long time ago there were moments when I thought I'd had feelings that went past friendship for him. Of course, I didn't. He was just one of the first men who'd ever been kind to me without wanting something in return.

Now we're close friends and coworkers, and he's happily married to a woman I absolutely adore.

A certain SEAL pops into my head. He hadn't wanted anything, had he? But I lied to him and ruined everything. I shove the thought away.

"Wanted to get a workout in before the meeting this morning."

He arches a brow. "Wanna try that again?"

I should have known better. We served together overseas, with me as a medic who saved his life on more than one occasion. I know he struggles with the weight of his past, too, though I imagine being married to his high school sweetheart has lessened a bit of it.

The two of them are perfect for each other, and if I ever hoped for that kind of connection, I might be jealous. "I couldn't sleep. But that's nothing new." Not one for vulnerability, I turn back toward the bag and slam my fist into it.

Michael comes around and holds the bag for me as I punch it, then spin and lands a kick. "If you want to talk about it we can."

"Nope. Not interested. Thanks though." With one final combination, I take off the gloves and grab my shaker bottle with the BCAA mixture I still haven't finished drinking. Amino acids first thing in the morning is a necessity when I'm hitting the gym, but I'm more than ready for coffee.

"Bianca, you can't keep it all bottled up."

"It's worked for me for the past thirty-five years," I call back as I head toward the door.

He chuckles, clearly understanding that the conversation is over. "See you in a bit."

"See you then!" I step out onto the street. The sky is darker than it should be, and I imagine it's due to the hurricane that's heading our way. The worst one Maine has seen in two decades, according to the newscasters.

Woohoo.

All around me, preparations are being made. Windows boarded up, furniture pulled from patios and hidden away inside. But I'm not worried. I've faced things far more terrifying than a hurricane and survived. And even if this is the thing that takes me out, well then, I guess I won't have to worry about much of anything anymore.

Slinging my backpack over my shoulders, I grip my cup and take off on the run that will bring me home. Since Hope Springs, Maine, is a small town, I run to the gym every morning as a warm-up, then use the three miles back to unwind after my workout.

I've made it a habit to push my body to its limits each and every day, never again wanting to be found unable to protect myself. Besides, it helps keep my anxiety at bay.

As it does every single year on this specific day, the darkness ebbs closer in my mind, but I shove it back. I won't let the past consume me. Never again. Especially not today.

My muscles are liquid by the time I reach the pier that sits beside Hope Springs' church. While I don't ever imagine I'll find myself going in for a Sunday service, I do stop at the pier and stare out over the sunrise.

Pale blue waters crash against the light sand as the world is painted in rays of purple, orange, and gold.

It's beautiful.

Even if I can't make myself believe in anything, I can believe that.

"Morning, Bianca." Pastor Redding comes to stand beside me. He's dressed in shorts and a T-shirt, his gray hair sweaty at the temples.

"Morning. Coming back from a run?"

"What gave it away?" he asks with a laugh.

I smile. Even if I don't occupy a pew every Sunday, I can appreciate the kindness of the man beside me. He's a good man. Good as they come. And he and his wife are staples in this tiny town that I now call home.

"Are you doing okay today?" he asks.

"Why do you ask?"

His expression reflects curiosity rather than judgment. But there's an understanding in his gaze that makes me feel…well, like he cares. Which is a new one for me. His wife has the exact same effect on me, and given that she owns the bakery in town, avoiding her is impossible.

I like cupcakes too much.

"God guided me to this pier this morning," he says. "I felt like I needed to run back by here rather than my usual route, and I can't help but believe that it's because you were going to be here."

"Listen, I appreciate you asking, but you know I'm not—"

"I know," he replies. "But even if you're unsure, He still knows and loves you."

The truth is, I don't know what I believe. But I've seen so much evil it's impossible for me to wrap my mind around the fact that there's a greater purpose to it all. "I'd like to believe that. I really would."

"Do you want to talk about what troubles you? Just friend to friend," he replies with a smile. "And it will never leave this conversation."

"Never?"

"Never," he replies.

I consider. Truth is, I wouldn't mind confiding in someone. I've always been too untrusting of therapists, and too nervous to make any friendships that go deeper than surface-level. I've learned that once you start digging, the past will bury you.

But since I trust the pastor, and I don't see what damage could be done if anyone ended up finding out, I shrug. "Today's my birthday," I reply. "And I haven't told anyone."

"Why not?"

"It doesn't feel like a day to celebrate," I admit. It's the day everything went wrong. The day my innocence was shattered, and I saw my life for what it was—a lie. A dangerous, blood-stained lie.

"Every birth is a miracle," he says. "So birthdays are

absolutely worth celebrating. Is there no one who knows? What about your parents?"

"Don't have them." It's not a lie, given they're both dead, but it still feels wrong.

"Well then." The pastor smiles at me. "Let me be the first to say happy birthday, Bianca. And while I will keep your confidence, you really should tell someone. You deserve to be celebrated. Even if it's just mentioning it to Kyra and letting her gift you one of her delicious birthday cupcakes."

I laugh. "Now there's an idea."

"Think about it," he replies with a kind smile.

I pull away. "Thanks, Pastor Redding. Have a good day."

"You, too."

"You deserve to be celebrated."

As I turn away, I can't help but remind myself that if he knew anything about me, he'd know just how false that statement is. Even a pastor would likely be disturbed by what he found lurking inside of me.

"Morning!" Lilly, the waitress and partial owner of Hope Springs Diner, greets me as she sets a mug of steaming coffee down in front of me. She sweeps her black hair off her shoulders and ties it back in a messy bun.

"Morning. You look rested."

She laughs, her bright blue eyes sparkling with joy.

"Baby finally slept through the night, and now I'm not entirely sure what to do with all of this energy I have."

I laugh softly. "Glad to hear it. He's a cutie. Alex brought him by the Knight Security office last week when he dropped off the coffee for our meeting."

She practically swoons where she stands. "He's perfect, and Sarah is just already such an amazing sister."

"She's a sweetie, too, so I can imagine."

A familiar ache in my chest blooms. I'd wanted kids at one point, but even as disappointed as I am, I try not to be bitter. Still, it's likely an impossibility, thanks to shrapnel I took in the abdomen during a patient transport overseas.

I suppose it just means that I get to spoil the children of my friends. Which is something that was also an impossibility until I'd moved here to Hope Springs after Lance Knight—a former Army Ranger I'd saved when we'd both been in the service—called me in to help track Michael after he'd gone missing.

Once I'd seen what Lance had built here, I knew I wanted to be a part of it. Even if I didn't ask to come work for him until a few months ago.

"You want your usual?" she asks.

"Pancakes, eggs, extra crispy bacon, and a side of crunchy peanut butter. You know me well."

Lilly grins and makes a note on the order pad she carries. "It's my job as both your friend and local diner owner. We'll get this right out." She turns and leaves the table, so I take a drink of my coffee and stare down at the e-reader I brought with me.

Some probably think I'm reading a pulse-pounding suspense.

Or a swoony romance.

But it's the Bible that is currently downloaded. I just don't want anyone to know that I'm searching for answers. For understanding. Because letting them know that means I also have to admit that I've found none.

That right now, it all just feels like words on a sheet of paper.

I turn it on and start reading where I left off in Exodus, but I haven't made it even a page when the bell dings over the front door.

I can feel him before I see him.

The blood-sizzling, bone-deep awareness that comes from being anywhere in Silas Williamson's vicinity.

The nightmares come flooding back.

Being lost in a hot jungle.

Closing up the same wounds over and over again because his skin was so tattered the stitches wouldn't hold.

"Bianca!" Little Eloise, his four-year-old niece, rushes over and wraps herself around my arm. I have to pull it free just to hug her back.

I force a smile, shoving the burdens of my past aside so I can focus on the beam of light that is Eloise Williamson. "Hey, sweet girl. How are you today?"

"You know, it's my birthday."

I grin at her as she smiles up with eyes that are so like Silas's, she could be his daughter. Likely because her mother was his twin. "Is it really?"

She nods. "I'm five today."

I give her a high five, happy that the one shining moment of today is that I get to share my birthday with such a wonderful little girl. "Happy birthday, kiddo."

"Thanks! When is your birthday?"

My gaze lifts to Silas. Aside from Pastor Redding now, he's the only one who knows...but does he remember? It was one of those things I told him about when we'd been in that jungle. When you think you may not survive to see another sunrise, the truth just kind of pours out.

Since he's not even looking at me, I'm assuming he doesn't remember—or doesn't care. "Today is your day, kiddo. Don't be worried about other people's birthdays, just focus on your own."

"Eloise, we need to get some breakfast before I drop you off at the library." Silas's deep voice resonates with a part of me that I try really, really, hard to separate from myself.

He makes me feel safe and scared.

Hopeful and hopeless.

Everything all at once.

All that I carry for him is a massive contradiction, but I know that's only because he knows everything the others don't. Secrets that I'd wanted to die with me in that jungle.

He could have buried me with them, but he's kept each and every one. Who knows why, and I'm honestly afraid to ask. So I just continue pushing forward, pretending that Silas Williamson doesn't hold the very keys to my heart. Keys that I gave to him when we'd been back in that jungle, barely surviving, with only each other to rely on.

Our connection is volatile now, but it wasn't always like that. Back then, he'd been everything to me. Honestly, he still is. No matter how hard I try to push him away.

I meet his gaze. "Good morning."

He grunts in response but doesn't speak to me. Silas is a man of few words, sure, but with me, he prefers to pretend I don't exist. I'm just glad he hasn't tried to keep Eloise and me apart. Losing her happy smile would break my already tattered heart.

"Can we eat with Bianca, Uncle Lassy? Please?" She puts her hands together and sticks her bottom lip out in a pout. "It's my birthday, please, please, please?"

He looks at me like he's hoping I'll tell her no, but I'm not that kind. "Okay. As long as it's okay with her."

"Fine by me. Come on, kiddo." I scoot over and she climbs onto the booth seat beside me.

"Morning, lovely!" Lilly greets, setting a coloring page and some crayons in front of her.

"Morning, Mrs. Phillips! It's my birthday!" Eloise greets.

"It is?" she exclaims, placing both hands on her hips and smiling widely. "Happy birthday, then! Special birthday pancakes coming right up."

"Yay!" Eloise claps her hands together and starts coloring as Lilly turns to Silas.

"Morning, Silas, what can I get for you?"

"Just coffee, thanks."

"No problem." Lilly leaves the table, and I pick up a crayon and start coloring the page alongside Eloise.

"Uncle Lassy is taking me to the arcade downtown. We're going when he's done with his meeting. It's going to be *so* fun because we're going to do the dance-off game. And Mrs. McGinley said I get to help her reshelve the books at the library while he's in his meeting! I love books." As Eloise keeps chattering happily, I sneak a peek at Silas, who's staring out the diner's window.

His expression is hard, uncomfortable, as it always is when we're near each other. Which makes it even more awkward, given we share either side of a duplex on the other side of town. A not-so-happy coincidence to be sure.

I know why he hates me.

I hate myself most days.

But it doesn't take away from the fact that I wish, for once, he'd look at me like he did all those years ago. Back before he knew the truth.

CHAPTER 3
Silas

"We have two installations this afternoon," Lance announces as he checks his clipboard. "Michael is flying out next week to head a protection detail in LA, and Jaxson will be out of town until the end of the month, though he's handling some of our digital work from his brother's house." He writes something on his clipboard, then sets it aside and withdraws some large black radios from a box beside him. "These will work if the cell towers go down with the hurricane. We have plenty of food, water, batteries, blankets, and medical supplies to help the town should we take the brunt of the storm."

"News said it will be hitting sometime tomorrow morning," Elijah says. "I helped Mrs. McGinley board up the library, and we've taken care of Doc's place and the church, too."

"Good." He turns to me. "You prepared?"

I nod.

"How about you?" he asks Bianca.

"I'll be getting my windows boarded up as soon as I get home," Bianca replies.

I have to force myself not to steal a glance at her. Just once. Sitting across from her this morning was torture because even as I despise everything she is and the lies she told me, I still find myself drawn to her.

Like a moth to a flame—she would destroy me, burning me up until there's nothing left but ash. If I ever let her that close again. Which I won't. Even I'm not that stupid.

"Great. Caleb is coming in for an onboard interview this afternoon. He's finally agreed to come on as one of our techs."

"Yeah?" Bianca sounds so thrilled I steal a glance at her now. She's beaming at Lance, her emerald eyes bright with joy. "That's wonderful!"

"He finally caved," Lance replies with a grin. "I've been trying to get him to come on—even just part-time—since he moved here."

Up until about two years ago, Caleb was living in the swamps of Florida, completely off-grid. That had come in handy when Michael had been shot. Reyna, Michael's now-wife, and Michael stumbled into his homestead, desperate for aid.

He'd been there to offer it, and we'd found them tended to and safe.

After that, he'd decided to leave the swamps and relocate here, though he maintains a good distance from most of the residents as he tries to acclimate to being around people again.

Still, he's a good man, and one I'd trust to have my back.

"Glad to hear he's coming in," I say.

"We're growing, that's for sure," Lance replies as he runs a hand through his auburn hair. "With the number of new clients we're taking on, as well as the monitoring for our current ones and the aid we lend to Sherriff Vick as needed, the help is definitely appreciated."

I doubt Lance ever thought his calling would turn into a large business like this, but it certainly has, and now Knight Security is the fastest-growing private security company on the East Coast.

"Elijah, any news to add?"

"Nope." The tech lead crosses his arms. "We've had a relatively quiet month, no break-ins, so nothing to report on that end."

"Good. Let's hope it stays that way." Lance sets the clipboard down. "All right, let's end in a prayer." He bows his head, and although I'm not a praying man, I do the same out of respect for my coworkers. "Dear Lord, we thank You for this day, for the ability to help others, and for Your guidance and discernment in moments of trial. Please be with us as we navigate this hurricane and keep us grounded in Your light. Please protect those in the path of this storm and guide us so we can help those who need it most. In Your holy name we pray, amen."

"Amen," Elijah and Michael reply at the same time.

"All right, hope you all have a great day. Silas, can I talk to you for a minute?"

In lieu of verbally responding, I push up from the desk I was leaning back on and walk over toward his desk. Elijah, Michael, and Bianca all clear out of the lighthouse, shutting the door behind them.

"You're on monitor duty today, huh?" I ask, dropping down into the chair beside his desk.

"That I am. At least for a few hours. After Caleb leaves, I'm headed home to be with Eliza and the baby. I'll be monitoring the systems from there."

"Nice. What's up?"

"I'll keep it brief since I know it's Eloise's birthday today."

"Appreciate it," I reply.

"I mainly just wanted to check in and see how you're doing. You've seemed a bit strained lately, and I wanted to see how I can help." I'm not surprised the former Army Ranger and captain sensed something was off. The man picks up on everything.

"Just settling in still," I reply. It's not a complete lie. Ever since Bianca moved here full-time and started working for Knight Security, it feels like someone pulled the rug out from under my feet. I'm still trying to adapt to seeing her every day.

But I can't tell Lance any of that because I've kept the fact that I know her a secret for many reasons. None of which I care to explain to him at the moment. Or maybe ever.

"You're sure that's all it is?"

"It is."

He nods. "Thanks for letting Eloise come to church with us yesterday. Did she have fun in Sunday school?"

"She did. Thanks for taking her. She's been asking to go but I just—"

"Couldn't make it," he interrupts, though his expression tells me that he knows it had nothing to do with couldn't and everything to do with wouldn't.

"Yeah. That's it," I reply, running a hand through my hair. "Is that all? I need to go pick her up and get her to the arcade before she drives Mrs. McGinley up the wall with questions."

Lance chuckles. "Sure thing. Let me know if you need anything, okay? I know you like to keep your personal life under wraps, but I'm here if you need me."

"Thanks. I know you are. See ya."

The sun is warm on my face as I walk down the steps of the lighthouse toward my truck that's parked in the lot. When Lance and I first met, I'd practically been dead. Bianca and I had just been rescued after spending a month running for our lives in the jungles outside Culvers' prison camp.

He'd been in the hospital after suffering his own near-death experience and happened to be walking past my room when he felt—as he calls it—drawn to come talk to me. He'd spoken to me about God, about faith, about surviving, and I'd struggled to have an open mind.

It didn't keep me from feeling my own draw toward him, though. He spoke with such confidence, such hope, that it lit a bit of my dark soul up. We'd gone our separate ways, but I always intended to catch up with him.

And then Sierra died.

The sudden passing of my twin sister and her husband Rick was another hit to my weary soul. It wasn't until I was back home in Texas that I found I'd been made guardian of Eloise.

At first, I'd said no.

I'd never even met the child. I'd hidden myself away in a mountain cabin in Montana, refusing to come see her even after she'd been born. Sierra was so upset at my staying away, but how was I supposed to explain the darkness in my soul? The weight that I carried? How could I have told her all the ways I struggled to cope with civilian life once I made it home?

It was when I went in to sign the papers to relinquish custody of Eloise that I'd felt someone—or something— knock the wind from my lungs. And as I'd paused, trying to catch my breath, I'd seen little Eloise sitting in a playpen at the children's services building, crying.

One look is all it took for me to realize what a mistake I was making by walking away. For all intents and purposes, I became a dad that day.

And I haven't looked back since.

I get into my truck and pull out of the lighthouse, making my way toward the bakery so I can pick up two cupcakes for Eloise and me tonight. I've had custody of her for three years now, and every year I've done my best to make her birthday special.

Since my parents are gone, Rick's too, it's just the two of us against the world.

Silas and Eloise.

And I'll die before I let anything happen to her.

So distracted by my thoughts, I didn't even notice Bianca's car sitting outside the bakery until I'm parked right alongside it. Dread burns a hole in my stomach, and I shift my truck into reverse, ready to bail, but when I see her sitting at a table in the corner, a single cupcake in front of her, I throw the truck back in park as memories assault me.

I know what today is for her.

It's Bianca's birthday, too.

And truth be told, I'm probably the only person in this town who knows it because she confessed to me that she hated today. That her birthday was the start of everything in her life falling apart.

She's in pain.

I slam my hands against the steering wheel as that realization hits me square in the gut. Leaning forward, I rest my forehead against the steering wheel between my hands. I can still see her, sitting on the jungle floor, her hair wet as rain poured down on top of us. The droplets on her cheeks were either rainwater or tears, who knows, but her pain—it hung heavy in the air around us.

So even though I don't want to, I get out of the truck and head inside. The tiny bell dings overhead, but Bianca doesn't look up.

Kyra Redding looks up from behind the counter and smiles at me. "Hey, Silas! I just finished Eloise's special cupcakes." She lifts a small white box and sets it on the counter.

"Thanks." Reaching into my pocket, I pull out some cash and set it on the counter as I take the box. "No change, thanks. You need help boarding up the windows?" I ask, noting the plywood leaning against the wall.

"I appreciate it, but my lovely husband and Henry Acker will be coming by to meet Felix. The three of them are putting them up."

"Have them call if you need additional hands."

"Will do." She beams. "Thanks." Her phone rings so she quickly excuses herself.

I glance over my shoulder at Bianca again. The cupcake in front of her is still untouched, undoubtedly lemon with white frosting and sugar crystals, as her mother used to make for her each year. There's a tablet in front of her and she's reading intently.

I don't know that she even realizes I'm here.

I could probably just slip out through the door—but when her brow furrows even further at whatever it is she's reading, and the small scar at the corner of her eye catches my attention, I'm thrown right back into that jungle.

I may despise what Bianca did.

But I cannot deny who she was to me.

So, I make my way over to her. "Enjoy your birthday."

She looks up at me now, green eyes full of surprise. "You know better than that."

"It's still your day."

"No," she replies, "it's not."

"Then what's with the cupcake?"

She looks down at it. "Tradition." Her gaze lands on the box in my hands. "Those for Eloise?"

"She wants spaghetti for dinner."

"Nice. Good meal."

"Yeah. Well. I'll see you around." I turn to leave, but as I'm doing so, I note a man standing across the street from the bakery.

He's not looking into the windows, but rather down at his phone. He's dressed casually in jeans and a gray T-shirt, but the gold watch on his wrist captures my attention. I can't make out the brand, but it's far too upscale for a man who dresses casually.

Alarm bells ring in my mind as the air around me shifts. Something is off.

"He's been out there all afternoon," Bianca says.

I look down at her, noting the worry on her face as she keeps her gaze focused on me. "You're afraid."

"Not afraid," she replies as she stands. "Just curious. Excuse me." Taking her cupcake and tablet, she leaves the bakery after waving goodbye to Kyra.

I remain where I am, watching the man with the golden

watch as he puts the phone up to his ear and starts walking—in the opposite direction of where Bianca went.

It could be nothing.

It's probably nothing.

But I can't shake the feeling that something other than a hurricane is heading to Hope Springs. Something that's been a long time coming.

CHAPTER 4
Bianca

Rain hammers down on top of us for the second time today, but it's a break from the stifling humid heat that's been nearly suffocating for the past few hours. My head aches, a throbbing that never seems to want to go away, but at least I'm alive.

Silas sits beside me in the little shelter we were able to find, a small outcropping of rock barely large enough for the both of us. The rain has washed away nearly all the blood and dirt that clung to his skin, revealing a muscled torso bearing bruises and injuries from his time in captivity.

He doesn't speak much, and I'm certainly grateful for that. Once I start talking, secrets may get spilled, and the man beside me might find out who he truly rescued.

As of now, I don't think he even has a clue that the woman he pulled out of this hell might as well be the daughter of a demon.

"Today's my birthday." I blurt it out. "I think."

"*What is today?*" *he asks.*

"*September seventh,*" *I reply.* "*If I've been counting the days right, which I may not have been.*"

"*September seventh,*" *he repeats.* "*Happy birthday.*"

"*No need to say that. I was just making conversation.*"

"*We should do something for your birthday.*"

I smile at him because it's impossible not to smile at Silas whenever he's looking at me like he is now. "*No, we shouldn't. I don't even like my birthday. I'm honestly not even sure why I said anything.*"

"*How do you not like your birthday?*" *he asks, then starts scooping mud from in front of us into a pile.*

"*It was the day everything fell apart,*" *I reply.*

"*What do you mean?*"

"*My mom died, and I ran away from home.*"

Silas stops scooping. "*I am so sorry, Bianca.*"

I shrug. It's a half-truth because the actual story is far more horrific. "*I just don't do much celebrating anymore.*"

"*What did you used to do? Before?*"

Leaning back against the rock, I try to decide how much to tell him. Truthfully, I never thought I'd ever want to speak about my past. Not after trying to keep it hidden for so long. But Silas makes me feel safe in a way I haven't felt ever since I was a little girl. And even then, I'd learned that security had been bought with the blood of innocent people.

Telling him doesn't feel like such a hard thing, especially given that I know our likelihood of survival is practically nonexistent. His wounds, despite my best efforts, are infected, and I'm nearly out of the supplies I need to keep it from spreading.

"My mom made me lemon cupcakes with vanilla frosting every year. She'd add sugar crystals to the top and we'd sneak out onto the roof and watch the sun go down while eating them."

"That sounds nice."

"It was," I reply honestly, then close my eyes as an onslaught of tears threatens. My mom had been my best friend. My rock. And the image of her body will forever haunt me. There's a part of me that almost wishes we won't make it out. Or at least that I won't. Because then I'll never have to suffer through these memories again. I'll be free of my past, blissfully unaware of the damage done.

"Well, it's no vanilla cupcake, but—" Silas trails off, and I open my eyes.

In front of me, shaped with dirt and leaves, sits a muddy cupcake, a single pink flower sticking out of the top. The tears fill my eyes again, and I look from it to the man sitting beside me. A Navy SEAL with a heart of gold. Far too good to be sharing air with the likes of me.

"It's perfect."

"Yeah?" he asks, mouth lifting at the corners in a boyish grin that seems far too light for our dark circumstances.

"Yeah." I reach forward and cup it in my hands, then close my eyes and blow the flower away as though I'm blowing out a candle.

"Happy birthday, Bianca."

"Thank you," I tell him, unsure how to explain that even though we'll likely die in this jungle, it's the best birthday I've had since I lost my mother.

THE MAN DIDN'T FOLLOW ME.

Something that puts me at ease, sure, but I'd almost hoped he was a threat so I could put some of this unrest to bed. It's been days of feeling as though I'm being followed but being unable to prove it.

Today was the first time I'd seen him.

Yesterday, it was a woman dressed in white capris and a black T-shirt who'd eyeballed me at the small market here in town. The day before that, it was a man wearing a suit and tie as he stood just outside the post office when I'd gone to collect my mail.

So either I'm being followed, or I'm losing my mind. Honestly, it could go either way.

I finish eating my cupcake, then set it aside and head into the kitchen to grab a glass of water. The small two-bedroom duplex I'm renting isn't much, but it's home. I even put pictures on the wall, something I haven't ever done before because I'd never planned to stay in one place long enough to get comfortable.

But I plan to stay here in Hope Springs as long as possible. Partly because I love it, and mainly because of the man currently making spaghetti on the other side of the duplex wall. It was a complete coincidence that I rented this place right after he did.

Even though I knew he wanted me to find somewhere else to live, I refused. Now I make an effort to leave before him and offset our schedules so we see each other as little as possible. For him and for me.

If I'd been anywhere else, I would have left at the first thought that someone could be following me. My father may be dead, but there are still people out there who were on his side. I know it. And if they find me, well, the jungle will look like a vacation in comparison.

I roll my shoulders and step out onto my half of the balcony that overlooks the ocean. The single chair and table I keep out here are inside the house in preparation for the storm, so I just lean against the railing. I should be inside, but with the windows boarded up, the house feels an awful lot like a prison cell, and I've spent enough time in those.

There's a good bit of distance between me and the crashing waves, but from here I can see the steadily darkening sky—a sign that the storm is getting closer. I feel a bit nervous knowing I have to go back inside, so I close my eyes and simply let myself *feel* the wind as it toys with my hair.

I let the freedom of my surroundings saturate my soul and alleviate some of the tension. And as I stand out here, I try to imagine that Jesus is standing with me. I try to picture Him, try to imagine what it would have been like to stand in His glorious presence.

And even though I'm struggling to connect with the Bible and God's Word, I try to pretend—for just a minute —that I'm not.

That it all makes sense and everything I've been through has brought me right where I am for a reason.

"You shouldn't be out here."

I jump, my heart racing as I whirl to the right and spot Silas standing on his side of the balcony, his arms crossed. "You're out here, too."

He doesn't respond, just starts to go back inside.

"I don't like feeling confined," I say quickly. Vulnerability is not something that comes easy to me, but I know that Silas will keep my secrets. Because he's done just that for half a decade already.

Silas pauses a moment, his large hand on the door. He looks like he wants to say something. And I wish he'd look at me.

Instead, he opens the door and says, "You'll be fine."

"Is this how it's going to be between us forever? We just don't talk about anything ever?"

"Yeah," he replies without hesitation. "Because as far as I'm concerned, we never knew each other, and what happened between us never happened." The door closes behind him.

How I ever thought things with Silas would get better, I'm not sure. I know he hates me. Despises that I settled here in Hope Springs. Maybe I should have left. Given him that distance he so clearly desires.

But how can I do that when it feels like things between us are unfinished?

I turn back toward the storm, trying my best to keep my head on straight. How is it that a hurricane doesn't scare me, but being inside a boarded-up house is terrifying?

THE WIND OUTSIDE IS DEAFENING.

I sit in my living room, knees curled up against my chest. Eyes closed. Just doing my best to keep breathing. I can't go outside because of the storm, and I can't seem to sleep because it's so loud in here I can barely hear myself think.

Then there's the panic attacks. The feeling of being smothered in this house. Like the walls are closing in around me. The wind echoes through my house like high-pitched screams.

Something hits the side of my house, and I bite back my own scream.

Eloise could be sleeping on the other side of the wall, and the last thing I want to do is wake her with my terror. I bite down on the inside of my cheek so hard that I taste the copper tang of my own blood.

Something hits my house again, this time above me.

Then a massive crack fills the house and the entire ceiling caves in.

I scream, lunging off of my couch just in time to avoid being crushed by the large tree that once stood outside my living room window.

It pins me, one of the branches catching my leg and holding me to the ground. I struggle to break free—heart pounding. This *cannot* be happening! Rain hammers down on me, soaking my pajamas and the carpet.

It's freezing, and I struggle to get free, but the pain in my leg shoots up through my body. Is this how I'm going to die? Pinned to the floor of my living room, being water-boarded by a storm?

"Come on!" I yell as I try to lift the tree off of my leg.

Another loud crack that sounds like thunder. I arch my back to tilt my head toward the front door as it flies open. Silas stands on the other side, soaked with rain water, his eyes wild and furious. He rushes forward and squats down to lift the branch off my leg, and I wiggle free.

Then, he kneels beside me, his hands running over my head, my arms, as he checks for injuries. "Are you all right?"

I look up at him and our gazes lock. For the first time, he's not looking at me like I'm an enemy. That mask he wears is gone, replaced with genuine concern. "I'm okay," I reply.

Silas stands, so I try to follow, but pain has me hissing through clenched teeth. One look down and I can tell that the branch tore through the sweatpants I'd been wearing and into the flesh of my leg.

Fantastic.

Here's hoping that won't need stitches.

"Come on." He lifts me and carries me out of my house and onto the front porch. A gust slams into us, nearly knocking him off of his feet. I can't hear a thing with the deafening wind and the boom of thunder.

We make it to his front door in seconds, but we're both soaked.

Still, at least his ceiling is relatively intact.

"Bianca!" Eloise screams and rushes toward me. She's wearing cartoon dog pajamas, her eyes red and full of tears. The room is dimly lit with a lantern since we lost power a few hours ago, and there's a stack of children's books on the coffee table.

"Hey, I'm good."

"You're hurt. Uncle Lassy, is she going to be okay?"

He sets me on the couch. "She'll be fine. I'll get the first aid kit." After setting me down, he heads down the hall. Eloise grabs a blanket and tucks against my side.

"I'll be perfectly fine, kid, I promise."

She sniffles. "It's so loud."

"I know, honey." I wrap an arm around her and press a kiss to the top of her head. I'm soaking wet, but she doesn't seem to mind, and neither do I. Truthfully, the closeness brings me more peace than I've had all night.

Which is insane, given the roof is literally caved in over my living room.

I glance up, grateful that the damage seems to be isolated to my half of the duplex.

Silas comes back down the hallway, still wearing his soaking wet clothes, and kneels in front of me.

"I can do it."

"You can't move," he whispers.

"I can—" But then I glance down at Eloise, who has

managed to fall sound asleep in the last sixty seconds. "Oh."

"I've been trying to get her to sleep all night." He lifts the blanket just enough to get a look at my leg, then proceeds to grip the tattered sides of my pantleg, and tear it away from the injury. "She's been up since the power went out." He studies my leg, so I take a moment to study him. Silas Williamson is stunning in his own right. Masculine, strong, his jaw sharp. The man commands attention when he walks in the room, even without trying.

I clear my throat. "How does it look?"

"Not too bad. Looks more surface." He opens a bottle of rubbing alcohol, then places a clean towel beneath my leg and pours the liquid onto the open cut.

I hiss through my teeth, doing my best not to make any noise or jarring movements that might wake Eloise up. Silas doesn't look up at me as he finishes cleaning, then wraps my leg in clean gauze and stands.

I watch him as he walks away, noting the way the muscles of his shoulders bunch as he moves. The man walks like a warrior. Like he's always one breath away from running into battle.

Outside, the storm rages on, but it's nothing compared to the one inside of me.

To keep myself from continuing to stare, I close my eyes and lean back, focusing only on Eloise's soft breathing and the sound of the storm.

It's a funny thing, but I don't feel nearly as suffocated in Silas's living room as I did in my own. Whether it's the man or exhaustion making me feel at peace, I'm not sure, but for the first time since the storm started, I feel the gentle fingers of exhaustion pulling me under, and I let them take me away from here.

Away from my past.

From the storm.

And from feelings better left buried six feet under.

CHAPTER 5
Silas

She's sleeping on my couch.

Looking absolutely stunning as she's cuddled next to my niece.

I stand at the kitchen counter, staring at them in the dim light of a lantern, as the storm dies down outside. They both look so peaceful, so utterly and completely quiet, and it infuriates me. Mainly because when I came back out and realized that Bianca had fallen asleep, I felt a bit of relief seeing her sitting there, knowing she was safe.

Which is ridiculous.

She's the last person I want getting close to Eloise.

Yet here we are. It wasn't me who put my little girl at ease, it was Bianca Theodore. A liar. A traitor. The daughter of a monster. Taking a deep breath, I lean my head forward and run both hands through my hair.

The black walkie-talkie sits silent on the counter, and since, according to my cell phone, we're coming up on seven thirty in the morning, I go ahead and grab it before retreating to my bedroom and turning it on.

Michael's voice is the first one I hear.

"We're running supplies to the church for those who had flooding, over."

"Awesome. I'm going to take a bag over to the library and leave it there, over," Lance replies.

I press the button. "Morning, team. Over."

"About time, sunshine! How did you make it through? Over."

Michael's tone is light and contrasts heavily with the darkness within me. "El and I are okay. Bianca had a tree collapse her roof last night and she was hurt, but it's just a surface wound. Over."

"She's okay? Over." Michael again, this time his tone all business.

"She is. Asleep right now. I'm going to head over in a minute and check on the damage. Over."

"I'll swing by as soon as I drop off the supplies at the church," Michael offers. "Lend a hand as I can. Over."

"That would be great, thanks. Over."

"I'll do the same," Lance says. "And we'll let Elijah know as soon as we hear from him. Check in at the top of the hour. Over."

"Confirmed. Over," Michael says, and I repeat it, then slip into some shoes and a sweatshirt before heading out into the living room. Eloise and Bianca are still asleep, so I pause for a moment to study them.

As she sleeps, Bianca's features are soft. Innocent.

She's beautiful. There's no question about that. Her eyes alone captivated me from the moment I first saw them. Is that why I'm so angry? Why I'm struggling so much to let the past go? Because I'd fallen in love with her so quickly that I hadn't seen the hit coming?

Forcing my attention away, I move toward the front door and unlock it, then pull it open. The sky is still overcast, but the rain and wind have stopped. The damage though—it's substantial. On our street, trees are down, cars pinned, houses damaged.

It could be worse, though.

Then I turn and look at Bianca's side of the duplex. Her front door is closed but not locked, so I push it open and step inside. Her carpet squishes beneath my boots, and I wince when I get a look at the ceiling.

Insulation and chunks of wood—both framing and tree in origin—litter the floor. It's caved in just over the couch, a large branch landing in the middle of her living room. The place is destroyed.

I head into her bedroom, knowing it's a mistake even before I cross over the threshold. She's everywhere in here. Her perfume lingering in the air, her blankets folded back like she's ready to climb into her bed.

Keep it together, Williamson. She's a viper, remember?

As soon as I've noted that it's still in one piece, thankfully, as is the rest of her house, I head back into the living room.

With the amount of damage in town, it could be weeks before she can get it completely fixed, but we can get it patched. That way it's at least livable in the meantime.

"Oh, boy."

I glance over at the door where Mrs. McGinley stands shaking her head. Caleb is beside her, his expression somber.

"How is the library and your house?" I ask.

"Better than this place." As our landlord, I imagine she's stressing over how she's going to get it fixed and when. "I'll make some calls. Is Bianca okay? I don't see her."

"She's asleep on my couch with Eloise. She hurt her leg, but otherwise is all right."

Her eyes widen and she looks up at the ceiling, then the couch beneath it. "She was in here when it fell?"

"How badly is she hurt?" Caleb asks.

"She's okay. It pinned her, but I got her out right after it fell. I heard her scream," I add quickly, not wanting the old woman to read into something that's not there. She's known in this town as a meddling matchmaker. The last thing I need is her trying to light a match that's been doused in gasoline.

"It's good you heard her, then. How's that sweet girl of yours?"

"Eloise is good."

"Well, you bring her by the library if you need to take care of anything. I'll make some calls and see what I can do about this. Caleb came and picked me up this morning so we could check all the properties."

Caleb nodded. "This is the worst of them, though. You'll want to get ahold of a contractor right away. There's likely other damage, too, and you may have a wait."

Perfect. "Honestly, I can handle the work." I'm not even entirely sure why I make the offer. The last thing I want to do is work closely with Bianca. And it's not as though I have the time. Not with everything else going on.

So what am I doing?

"You sure about that?" she asks.

I guess I am now. "It'll save you money on the fix, and I used to work contracting with my dad when he was still around. I can do it."

"Well, you're hired. But you're going to let me pay you for your time too."

"If you could just reimburse the supplies and keep Eloise while I work on it, that would be a fair trade."

"Consider it done." She holds out a hand so I walk over and take it. "Let me know what you need."

"I'll just make a list of supplies and head over to Felix's. I can bring you receipts."

"Have him put them under my account," she says. "Anything you have to go somewhere else for, I'll reimburse you directly."

"Sounds great to me. Thanks."

"Boy, don't thank me. Thank you. I better get back to the library, Lance is heading over with some supplies."

"Let me know if you want an extra set of hands," Caleb offers.

"Will do. Thanks. Are the roads drivable?"

"Barely," she replies. "People have been out clearing the roads since the storm broke early this morning, so they're getting there. I got word that the power should be back on in—" As soon as she says it, Bianca's porch light comes on. Mrs. McGinley beams. "Well, would you look at that. We have power. Thank you, Jesus." She closes her eyes, then reopens them and smiles at me. "Call if you need anything, and let me know when you'll be bringing that sweet girl over."

"Probably in an hour or so, if that's okay."

"That's perfect. See you then." She smiles and heads down the porch steps with Caleb at her side.

They're just reaching the curb when Michael pulls up in front of the house on his motorcycle. He removes his helmet and places it on the tank, then comes up the steps. "This looks rough." He whistles. "Where's B?"

"Asleep on my couch with Eloise," I tell him, trying to ignore the way he arches a brow. "The tree fell on her, so I brought her over there to take a look at her leg, and they fell asleep."

"I bet they were exhausted. Lot of activity. At least the storm wasn't as bad as they were predicting." Michael steps into the living room. "But there were quite a few houses that took hits like this."

"I told Mrs. McGinley I'd handle the work. I can get it patched by tonight, then do the rest of the work over the weekend."

"You moonlighting as a handyman?" he asks.

"Something like that," I reply. My cell rings. "Guess

service is back." I check the readout and see it's Elijah. Pressing the phone to my ear, I answer, "Williamson."

"You with Michael?"

"Yeah."

"Good, saves me a call. I need you both at the lighthouse. Bring Bianca if you can. We've got a potential situation."

"What is it?"

"I'd rather tell you in person. Sheriff Vick will be meeting us here, too, and he's got some information, too."

"Okay. Be there soon." My stomach churns with unease. What could it be? Was there more damage? Someone missing? "They want us at the lighthouse. Seems there's an issue."

Michael's expression mimics the one I know is on my face. "He didn't say what?"

I shake my head. "Just that Sheriff Vick is involved."

SINCE IT'S BIANCA'S RIGHT LEG THAT GOT HURT, I OFFER TO drive. Logically, I know her wound wasn't even deep enough to need stitches, but I'm still so shaken. Her scream still echoes through my mind. And seeing her pinned beneath that branch, the storm pouring into her house… it's still too fresh.

After dropping Eloise off with Mrs. McGinley, we pull up in front of the lighthouse. Bianca hasn't said much this morning, and I haven't exactly been interested in striking up a conversation.

Words don't come easily to me, they never really have. Sierra was always the talker. She could make a friend out of anyone. But my lack of conversational abilities are even worse when I'm around Bianca. Likely because I'm constantly on guard, watching what I say.

Before I'm even out of the truck, she's opening her door and limping up to the front door of the lighthouse. I follow, keeping my distance, but rushing around to pull the door open for her.

"Thanks," she mutters.

Inside, Lance, Elijah, Michael, and the sheriff are waiting. "Sorry we're late, I had to drop Eloise off."

"No problem. How's the leg?" Sheriff Vick asks.

"Not the worst thing I've dealt with," Bianca replies as she leans back against a desk.

If only they knew how true that was.

"So what's going on?"

Sheriff Vick reaches into a manila folder and withdraws a photograph. "Any of you recognize this man?" he asks, showing us the photograph.

I recognize him instantly.

As I know Bianca does.

"He was outside the bakery yesterday," I tell them.

"You saw him?" the sheriff asks.

"I did too," Bianca adds.

"Who is he?"

"We found his body this morning. We initially thought

he might be a tourist who got caught up in the storm, but unless hurricanes are shooting people at point-blank range these days, he was killed before or during. We'll know soon enough."

"Someone killed him?" Bianca asks.

Her face is pale.

I flex my hands, wanting to reach out and offer some sort of comfort, but know that I have no business doing so.

"Yes. Normally I wouldn't involve you guys in this, but I think I might be in over my head. I did some digging, and there was more than one red flag that went up. One in particular connects to a crime boss who's been dead for quite a while now. It's all in the folder," he says.

Bianca's entire body goes rigid, and she begins to breathe heavily.

Even though it goes against my own self-preservation, I reach out and cover her hand with mine. The action doesn't go unnoticed by the others, but Bianca doesn't flinch. It's as though she can't even feel the touch.

Sheriff Vick continues, "I'm not sure why he's here or who killed him, but if there's even the possibility of a crime syndicate setup up shop in Hope Springs, I want to know about it."

"We can definitely get you some answers, Sheriff," Elijah says as he takes the offered manila folder.

"I would appreciate it." He sighs. "These last few years have been stressful. I think I may need to retire soon." He smiles, then leaves the office.

As soon as the door shuts behind him, all eyes shift to Bianca.

"Is there something we need to know?" Lance asks.

Bianca doesn't respond. She's so pale I worry she might pass out, and her eyes are still staring straight ahead, her breathing faster than it should be.

"Bianca." I say her name, hoping to break through.

She shifts her gaze to me, green eyes wide and terrified. "He can't be alive, Silas. I killed him."

CHAPTER 6
Bianca

"**I**'m sorry, who did you kill?" Michael asks.

"What's the name of the crime boss the sheriff mentioned?" Silas asks, releasing my hand. I hate that he let me go. His touch kept me grounded as I mull over the fact that the very thing I've been afraid of is happening right before my eyes.

Why are they coming for me now?

Elijah opens the folder and checks it. "Lucian Culvers. That guy was bad news. I remember hearing about him back when the military was looking for intel on his overseas operations."

The name is acid to my ears, searing me from the inside.

"What's going on here?" Lance asks, looking from me to Silas. I keep waiting for Silas to start spilling my secrets, but even after everything, he's waiting for me to confess.

For me to speak the truths I've been running from for decades.

I would love to keep the secrets longer. Forever, really. But if the fight is here and my entire team is involved, I can't keep them in the dark. Even if it means they send me packing. Which they honestly should do. If I'm here, I'll only bring danger to their doorsteps.

"Lucian Culvers was my father." Just speaking the words makes my stomach burn. I want to vomit, scream, cry, and run away. But I can't do any of it. I *won't* do it. Not anymore.

"This guy?" Elijah asks, tapping the folder. "This guy who ran drugs, money, guns, and people all over the world? The same Culvers who took out nearly an entire team of Navy SEALs sent to stop him?"

"Yes," I reply, unwilling to look at Silas.

"The same one who held you captive?" Lance asks Silas.

A muscle in his jaw tightens. "One and the same," Silas replies.

Lance leans back against a desk and crosses his arms. "Rescuing Michael was not the first time you two had met."

It's not a question, and even though we didn't outright deny it, our secret still counts as a lie. "No, it wasn't. I first met Silas when he rescued me from a death sentence at my father's camp in the jungles of Cambodia."

"I'm sorry—*what?*" Michael demands, his temper flaring.

"Michael," Lance starts.

"No, don't *Michael* me. They lied. I want the whole truth. All of it. Now. What does your dad have to do with our dead guy, and why are they here now?"

"On my seventeenth birthday, my father discovered that my mother was planning to run away with me. He killed her for it, and I witnessed the whole thing. As soon as I could, I stole money and ran, then paid someone to erase me from existence and turn me into Bianca Theodore."

There's so much more to the story that I'm leaving out. Darkness that I can't bear to speak out loud. Not ever. It will suffocate me if I let it, and speaking it aloud will surely release pain I've kept buried for as long as possible.

Elijah clicks away on his keyboard, then turns to me. "Props to whoever did the wipe and identity setup. It's solid."

"Of course you're giving her a compliment right now." Michael rolls his eyes.

"I'm merely mentioning that the check is solid. I didn't catch anything when I looked into her before we hired her."

"The military didn't catch anything either when she joined," Michael reminds him.

Elijah shrugs. Everyone in this room knows he's more thorough than even the United States military when it comes to background checks. Elijah can find a speck of dust in a digital haystack.

Lance remains silent. I meet his gaze. Will he fire me?

Throw me out of here without another look? He's a man of God. Honest to his soul. What will he do with someone like me, who's been lying about who she is for years?

"I'm sorry I didn't say anything. I'm so sorry I kept it a secret. I just—I didn't think it would be an issue."

"What do you mean, you killed him?" Michael asks. "Can we get back to that?"

I close my eyes momentarily, memories of my abduction and the botched surgery rushing back. "I was grabbed from a military base in Afghanistan," I tell them. "Taken by someone my father paid. They knocked me out and flew me to his secret camp in Cambodia because he was dying and needed surgery to remove a blockage in his gut. There were complications, and I didn't save him. I could have. And I chose not to."

Beside me, Silas remains silent. He's heard this before. Then, we'd both been staring down the barrel of weapons as we knelt on the soft, jungle dirt. But one glance at him and I see it's not any easier to digest this time around.

Michael studies me. "So you didn't actively murder someone, you just refused medical care."

"I could have saved him," I insist, not wanting Michael to soften what I did. "I was good at what I did. But I saw an opportunity to rid the world of a monster, and I took it." The room is silent, no one wanting to say what's on their mind. I can feel the disappointment. The anger. The repulsion. It's the same way it felt when Silas found out the truth. That the man who'd killed his friends and tortured him was the same man I used to call my dad. The same one who used to tuck me in at night. Who cradled me when I'd been an infant.

Tears burn in my eyes, but I struggle to keep them hidden. "Look, I'll leave. They'll follow." I start toward the door.

"No." A single word spoken by a man shouldn't hold such power. But when spoken by Silas Williamson, and directed at me, it does.

I stop moving and turn to face the room.

"You've been running your entire life. They're here now. And they'll come after all of us simply because we associated with you. It would be foolish to think that leaving will draw them away from here. They'll just assume we know where you are and use us to find you."

"But you won't know where I'm going."

"You and I both know that won't stop them from trying to figure it out."

Torture. He's talking about torture. Bile burns my throat.

I think about everyone here that I've come to care for. Lance and his wife, Eliza, Michael and his wife, Reyna, Elijah and his wife, Andie, Lilly, Alex, Pastor Redding, Kyra...Silas and Eloise. The list goes on and on. Would running really put them in more danger?

And if leaving will cause pain, then what does staying risk? Either way, it seems I'm risking nothing short of everything.

"If your fa—Culvers is dead," Michael starts, "then who's coming after you now?"

"My uncle, River, would have taken over the organization after the death of Lucian," I reply. "He's not quite as bloodthirsty, though just as dangerous. Even more so, maybe, because he's less predictable."

"Why would they be coming after you now?"

"They want me dead. My father's group has their own brand of justice they like to dole out. I've been running ever since I was pulled out of that jungle."

"Why didn't you change your name after the rescue?" Elijah asks. "You clearly had someone who could do it for you, why not do it and disappear?"

Because Silas wouldn't be able to find me. It's not like I can speak that truth out loud, though. Silas made it clear he wanted nothing to do with me, but I always hoped that maybe if he changed his mind— "I was attached to the name," I reply. "And I thought they would be so busy with the organization falling apart around them that they wouldn't be focused on me."

"Well, you were wrong," Michael says. "And now they've come to Hope Springs."

"I know. Sorry doesn't cut it, I know that, but I never would have come here if I thought the danger was still relevant."

His gaze darkens. "You're the daughter of one of the most dangerous men the United States has ever seen, and —to top it off—you let him die on an operating table. Why would you think the danger would ever disappear?"

It's a fair question, and one I can't blame Michael for asking. Everyone he loves lives here in Hope Springs. His wife, parents, sister, nephew, friends—they all reside in this town. If anyone were to threaten these people I care about, I would fight to the death for them.

It makes me despise myself a bit more. And I didn't think that was possible.

"I'm sorry," I repeat. "Tell me what to do and I'll do it."

Michael sighs. "The danger isn't the problem. We've all faced down our fair share of enemies. It's the hidden truths I have a problem with."

"Same," Elijah adds.

Lance remains quiet. I'm not sure how, but his silence is even more deafening than Michael's harsh words.

"Lance, if you want me gone, just say the word. I'll go."

His gaze flicks from me to Silas, then back to me. "No. You're our family now, Bianca. And you've saved our lives before. Now it's our turn. But we need complete honesty from here on out. No more secrets."

No more secrets. "I carry so many of those, I'm not even sure where to start unraveling them," I reply truthfully.

Lance nods in understanding. "Start with any known names of those who may be on your uncle's payroll."

BY THE TIME I'VE FINISHED LISTING OUT THE NAMES OF everyone I remember from my father's organization, I'm beyond exhausted. Silas and Michael left shortly after I started listing names, leaving Lance to take notes and Elijah to work on running backgrounds.

They were still working when I left, and even though I would love a hot shower and to crawl into bed, going home to a massive hole in the roof of my house is far too depressing for me.

I tell myself that's why I'm standing outside the church just past nightfall.

But even I know it's another lie. The truth is, after a day of ripping open old wounds, I'm desperate for answers. And I'm not sure I can get them anywhere else.

In fact, I *know* I can't get them anywhere else.

The front door opens and Pastor Redding steps out. He starts to lock up behind him, then seems shocked when he catches sight of me standing on the front steps. "Bianca, this is a great surprise."

"How do you know?"

He shoves his keys back into his pocket. "How do I know what?"

"That God is up there. That He's listening? That He cares? How do you know any of that is the truth?" My chest is heavy, the questions suffocating me.

Pastor Redding smiles softly at me and opens the door, then gestures for me to step inside. "Come on in, child, let's talk."

I should walk away. Leave him here in the church and head home. But I can't ignore the feeling in my chest that tells me to take a step forward. Then another, and another, until I'm walking into the sanctuary.

Straight ahead is a cross. And the moment my gaze lands on it, the tears spill from my eyes as exhaustion nearly takes me to my knees. "I'm so tired," I tell him. "I'm so tired of all of it."

"Then come and find rest." He wraps an arm around my shoulders and guides me toward a pew in the back where we both sit.

"I'm sorry," I whisper between the tears. "It's all just so heavy. Life. Pain. Why is living so hard?"

"Don't apologize," he replies. "Not to me. Take all the time you need."

"All my life I was told I was strong. My mother told me that all growing up. That I was stronger than I ever knew. That I could carry anything if only I put my faith where it belongs. She was a believer, yet she married a monster."

"Sometimes people make bad decisions," Pastor Redding replies.

"She had to have known who he was before she married him. And then he—" I close my eyes. "My father was a terrible man, Pastor. He did awful things, and I was so blinded by the money he had, by the material possessions he granted me, that I didn't even bother to try and see through it."

"But you see through it now."

"I've seen it for a long time," I admit. I turn to him, tears still blurring my vision. "I've been reading a Bible on my tablet. Searching for answers. But I don't feel Him. Why can't I feel God?"

"The fact that you're trying to feel Him tells me you do. Your heart is burdened with the weight of your past. If you want to truly move into your new life, then you have to accept your Savior, ask for forgiveness, and let the past go."

"Forgiveness." I shake my head. "I'm not deserving. You have no idea the things I've seen. The poison in my blood."

"None of us are deserving," he tells me. "Jesus didn't die for us because we were worthy. He died for us out of love."

"Love is another fallacy in my world, Pastor."

"It's not a fallacy in anyone's world," he replies. "You just need to open your heart to receive it."

CHAPTER 7
Silas

It's nearly ten and she's still not home.

Where is she? Where could she have gone?

Eloise is sleeping soundly on my side of the duplex, as evidenced by her soft breathing through the baby monitor on my hip. Using a bright work light, I apply another coat of putty to Bianca's ceiling.

It took most of the day, but Felix, the hardware store owner, and his son-in-law Alex came to help. We were able to clear the tree from Bianca's house, got the roof closed up, and now the ceiling has been patched with sheet rock.

I glance out the open front door again. Did River's people find Bianca? Is she gone? I climb down from the ladder, then head out onto the porch, closing the door behind me. As soon as I'm sitting, I take a drink from my bottle of water.

If I had her number, I could call her. But I didn't allow

myself to put it into my phone even after she started work at Knight Security.

The last thing I wanted was another piece of her tied to me. She already has so much of me it's sickening.

Now I wish I had the number, if only to make sure she's still here in Hope Springs.

Honestly, it's more than likely she ran. Took off into the distance, just as she did all those years ago. Even as the thought graces my mind, a pair of headlights turn down our street.

She comes to a stop in front of her house and climbs out, a book in her hand.

"Hey."

"Hey." I don't look up at her even as she takes a seat on the steps in front of her front door. It's then I glance over at her. "Been at the library?"

She looks down at the book in her hands. "The church. It's the Bible. Pastor Redding gave it to me."

"A Bible? I didn't take you for a believer."

"Getting there," she replies with a soft smile. "I'm trying to find my way to Him."

I grunt in response. Truth is, I hardened my heart against faith after my sister's death. Before then, I believed, sure. Though I never practiced my faith. Never prayed. Never spent a Sunday in a pew.

Not until I got the call that my sister had been in an accident.

I prayed then.

But she stayed dead.

And I haven't dropped to my knees since.

"I'm sorry that I came to Hope Springs and that I stayed. It was never my intention to bring danger to this town."

"Then what was your intention?" I ask. "Why did you stay?"

"The truth?"

"Would be nice for a change."

"You." The single word carries far more weight than I think she realizes.

"Me."

"Yes. Things were so strained between us after—"

"We nearly died and you bailed the moment you got the chance?"

She shakes her head, and I note that she runs her fingers over the pages of the Bible. Does it bring her comfort to do that? "I thought that if I left, you'd find peace. I was worried they'd track me down and if I was near you—they weren't after you."

"They were after both of us," I remind her. "I escaped, too."

"But I was—"

"I know who you were," I snap. "Who you are." My tone is harsher than I mean it to be, so I take a deep breath. I'm not out here to argue. To let her defend a position I've been aware of since that day in the jungle. Truth is, in her shoes, I don't know that I would have been upfront either. But it still stings.

Each and every moment we spent together in that

jungle, running for our lives, is branded in my brain. And somehow, the worst of it wasn't the pain or the hunger. It was finding out that the woman I had fallen in love with wasn't who I thought she was.

That she'd been lying to me from the start.

"You mean a lot to me, Silas. I know that you'll never want to be friends, but I needed to be near you. I can't explain it. But it's the truth."

Her words are a gauntlet crashing down on top of me. Both relief and pain resonate through me, and I can't tell which is the better feeling. "I don't trust you, Bianca."

"I know you don't."

"And that's not going to change." I meet her gaze now. Her gorgeous emerald eyes that haunt my every waking hour. "Ever."

They fill with tears, and she nods.

Desperate for distance between us, I stand. "Your ceiling is patched. I'll finish up the framing tomorrow."

She stands. "My ceiling—you worked on my ceiling."

"Mrs. McGinley let me in because I told her I'd fix the damage so she didn't have to wait for a contractor."

Her expression softens. "Thank you."

"I did it for her. Not you." But we both know that's not true. My gaze dips to her lips. To the mouth I tasted briefly all those years ago, and the affection I still carry—even as I wish I could have ripped it out of my heart by the roots— springs to life.

"I appreciate it anyway."

"Yeah. Well—"

"I gave Lance that list of names he was looking for," she interrupts.

"Good. Then they'll find him in no time, I'm sure." I turn away.

"I loved you, too, Silas."

I freeze in place, her words carving away at my walls. "Which makes what you did even worse. Goodnight, Bianca."

I come awake at the sound of a branch snapping. Bianca is sleeping only a few feet away from me, her breathing soft.

But I know I heard something.

Gripping the scalpel I've been carrying since our escape, I roll up to the balls of my feet, then creep off to the side. Two men move through the jungle, dressed head-to-toe in tactical gear. If it weren't for the armbands around their biceps, they could have been friendlies here to find us.

But the black diamond sigil on their armbands is that of Lucian Culvers. The very man who'd captured me and killed my entire team.

My hand tightens around the handle of the blade, but I remain hidden. They may just move past us...but Bianca whimpers in her sleep, something she does rather regularly due to nightmares.

The men hear her, and they raise their weapons, then turn toward where she sleeps. I have mere seconds to react before they break through the brush that serves as our shield.

She whimpers again.

"Come on out here, sweetheart, we won't hurt you," one man calls out, then grins at the other. "Much," he adds.

They take another step.

Then another.

I lunge, slamming my body into the first man and taking him to the ground. "Run!" I bellow, hoping she hears me so at least one of us gets away. Maybe that's my purpose in all this, to get her free so she can do good in the world.

I slam my fist into the man's face, but the second man is faster. He slams the stock of his weapon into my head and my vision goes blurry. I fall over to the side and Bianca slides to her knees beside me.

"There she is. Little princess."

Bianca straightens. "You will not hurt him."

"Or what?"

She raises the scalpel I hadn't realized she'd picked up from the ground and presses the blade to her throat. "I'll take away my uncle's ability to get revenge. Isn't that what you're after?"

"What are you talking about?" I ask as I try to sit up. The world around me spins, and the pain is nearly blinding.

"Stay down," Bianca tells me as the man I'd tackled aims his weapon right at me. And as I sit here, staring down the barrel of a loaded weapon, I'm hit with the realization that I've been on the run with a woman I know nothing about.

"Who are you?"

"You don't know?" the first man says with a laugh. His beard is graying, his eyes hard and amused all at the same time.

"You've been running around with the daughter of the very man who killed all your buddies."

SLEEP DIDN'T COME LAST NIGHT.

I tried. I counted sheep, the fan blades as they whirred around above my head, I even turned on white noise on my phone to see if it would help slow my brain down. But all I could think of was Bianca's words over and over again.

"I loved you too, Silas."

Love. What a joke. I'd fallen for her, sure, but we'd been starving, exhausted, in pain, unsure if we'd live to see another sunset. It took time for me to realize that it hadn't been actual love. I'd just been too stupid to see it then.

I pour another mug of coffee and down the dark liquid as I watch Eloise play happily with her dolls.

She turns toward me. "Uncle Lassy?"

With a smile on my face, I carry my coffee into the living room, then set it on the end table as I take a seat on the couch. Eloise kneels on the floor between the couch and the coffee table, a pile of dolls in front of her.

"What is it, Nugget?"

Eloise holds up a doll that's half-dressed with what I can only imagine is supposed to be a silver ballgown. "I can't get her dress on," she says, holding the doll out for me. I take the doll from her and work the dress up over the top of her, then Velcro it in the back. When I hand it back to Eloise, she's beaming at me like I'm her hero.

"You're the best, Uncle Lassy," she says, happily taking the doll and adding her to the collection of other dressed dolls on the table.

Uncle Lassy. No matter how many times I hear it, it never gets old. The power this little girl has over me is endless. No matter how poor my mood is, one smile from her and it's instantly lifted.

"I try. So where are they all going?"

"A fancy party," she replies. "Like the one we had for Jaxson and Margot."

"A wedding, then?"

She shakes her head. "No, not a wedding. It's *like* the one they had, but not exactly." She uses a small hairbrush to smooth the blonde strands of doll hair. "No one is getting married, they just met!"

"Ooh, okay. I gotcha."

As I reach over for my mug, my gaze lands on a picture of my sister and her husband. My heart aches at the sight of my twin sister smiling widely, her husband right beside her. Eloise may never get the chance to meet her parents, but I'm going to make certain she recognizes them.

My sister would have wanted that.

I may not be a praying man, but I do hope that wherever she is, Sierra knows just how much I love her little girl.

The doorbell rings, startling me out of my reminiscing.

My heart thuds in my chest, faster than normal, and on

instinct, my hand goes to my lower back where the large knife I always carry is sheathed. It doesn't matter how long I've been home, I still fear not knowing who's on the other side of the door.

Especially now, knowing who's coming after Bianca. Given that I let her out, it's possible they're coming for me, too.

After checking the peephole, I drop my hand from the knife and open the door. Lance stands on the other side, his auburn hair shining in the bright sun. He's dressed in work jeans that are stained with paint from who knows when and a blue flannel with a white shirt underneath. It's his typical handyman clothing, which likely means he's either here to offer me help or he's stopping by on his way to another job.

"Morning," I greet.

"Morning. Can I come in?"

"Sure thing." I step aside, and he comes in.

"Lance!" Eloise leaps up from where she sits on the floor and rushes forward to jump into Lance's waiting embrace.

"Morning there, little El! How are you this morning?"

"Awesome. I slept *soooo* good," she says, stretching out the 'so.'

"I'm glad to hear it." He releases her and stands. "Can we talk?"

I nod. "Coffee?"

"That would be great, thanks."

I head into the kitchen and he follows. After filling a

mug with fresh coffee, I offer it to him, then lean back against the counter. "If this is about Bianca, I'm sorry for not telling you sooner. It wasn't my story to tell."

"I get that." He takes a seat at the counter. "I do wish you would have told me, as a friend, but I can understand why you didn't. What I want to know is how deep your connection to her runs."

I should have seen this coming. "You're worried they're coming for me, too?"

"I'm worried your head is clouded. I want to make sure it's clear."

"It's clear. Whatever was between us all those years ago is gone. I feel nothing for her."

"Even nothing is something," Lance replies.

"Not this time. Bianca lied to me. I don't have tolerance for people who do that."

"So you have no feelings for her whatsoever? When she walks in the room, your gaze isn't immediately drawn to her?" When I don't immediately answer, he continues, "Because I also don't care to be lied to."

Defeated, I run a hand through my hair. "Whatever is still there is only lingering feelings that haven't burned off yet."

"What happened to you two in that jungle?"

"She didn't tell you?" I assumed that after I left yester-day, she'd told them everything. About what a sucker I was for my feelings and how easily I'd fallen.

"No. And I didn't ask. I am asking you. As your friend

and someone who wants to make sure you're both operating with full transparency."

I sigh, knowing I owe him an explanation. After checking to make sure Eloise is distracted with her dolls, softly humming to herself as she has them dance around, I lean in and lower my voice. "When I was being held, I'd come to the understanding that I was going to die. I knew it without a second thought, that each time they came to pull information from me could be my last. And then, one night, a man showed up in my cell. He told me that he was there to rescue me, but that he couldn't guide me out. He told me which direction to run and that the door would be unlocked. Then he unshackled me. And as soon as I could stand up, he slipped out." I remember the day like it was yesterday—the stench of the cell, the sound of water dripping down the stone walls…the feel of my bare feet against the concrete floor. "As I was leaving, I heard a woman yell right before two of Culvers' guards came out. They were going to kill her, I knew that much, and I had this feeling that I needed to save her, too. That I needed to get her out. So I did."

Lance remains silent as I finish up my coffee and pour another cup, topping off his as well.

"I was injured badly, and she stitched me up a couple times. We ran for weeks. Living off of what game we could find and whatever fresh water we managed to get ahold of. It was just the two of us for weeks," I tell him. "Feelings were bound to blossom. We kissed. Once. Then two guards found us and nearly killed us before my cousin's search and rescue team showed up to rescue us."

"I remember you saying your cousins pulled you out."

"They'd just gotten their company off the ground, and we were their first rescue." My cousins—five brothers on my mom's side—opened up their own search and rescue company out of Texas. They find what no one else can, and my sister had them looking for me.

"So they pulled you out."

"Right after I'd found out that the woman I'd been protecting, the one I rescued, was the daughter of the same man who slaughtered my entire team and tortured me for weeks."

"Bianca didn't get to choose her father."

"No," I admit. "But she could have told me."

Lance considers. "What would you have done, if you'd known who she was? Would you have left her there to die?"

Save her. Even now the words come rushing back to me. "No. I would have pulled her out anyway."

"And if she'd told you after you rescued her. Would you have killed her for who she was?"

I think that's what stings the most, though, is that even after the weeks of us being together, of my protecting her and us relying only on each other, she still didn't trust me enough to tell me. "No."

"Look, Bianca grew up in a world that was kill or be killed, yet when it came down to surviving or taking the easy way out and remaining with her father, she chose to leave and survive on her own. I'm not saying what she did was right. I'm not a fan of lies, but forgiving her is going to be the first step in moving forward."

"I'm working on it."

"I know you've struggled with your faith for a long time, but if you want to pray about it, I'm here."

There's a heaviness that settles over my heart that I can't explain, so I rub the palm of my hand against my chest. "I don't."

"When that changes, I'll still be here."

CHAPTER 8

Bianca

ONE WEEK LATER

A fresh coat of paint always feels like such a victory. And rolling the final coat of paint over my ceiling feels good. It's been a week since it caved in on me, and the repair is finally finished, thanks to Silas and Felix. They've been working practically nonstop. Lance helped as he could, as did Michael and Elijah, but most of the work has definitely been Silas.

He's up on a ladder now, fixing a recessed light that was damaged during the storm, and I have to actively force my attention away from him. The man captures my attention unlike anyone else.

I've even been praying about it.

Asking for guidance when it comes to my feelings for him. And even though I've gotten a lot closer to God since Pastor Redding gave me the old, worn Bible I've been studying, there still hasn't been a clear answer.

But I keep praying while I focus on rebuilding myself

as a woman of faith. Honestly, I've been praying about everything lately. Every time a thought enters my mind that makes me anxious or angry, I pray.

Letting go of the anger is a big one for me, and while I'm still not there yet, I know I'm getting closer. I can feel that my heart is lighter, my soul less weary.

"Done." Silas climbs down the ladder and sets the now empty box on the counter.

"Looks good, thanks."

He grunts and starts collecting his tools, placing them in an orange box. He pauses a moment, gaze locked on the Bible sitting open on my counter. "Still reading it?"

"I am."

"Have you found whatever it is you're looking for?" His tone is casual, but I get the sneaking suspicion that he's prying for more. That he's genuinely curious. It makes my heart leap with joy.

"Getting there," I tell him. "I've found a lot more than I ever did on my own."

Silas grunts again and lifts the toolbox as he heads for the door.

"Oh, listen, now that it's done, I was thinking I could make dinner for you and Eloise? As a thank you."

Silas turns to me. "I don't need a thank you."

"I know you don't, but I would still like to do it. I was even going to invite the others over, too. Lance, Eliza, Michael, Reyna, Andie, and Felix. Elijah's on duty tonight, but I was planning to take a plate over to him later."

"A dinner party."

"Basically." Nerves twist in my gut. "I've never hosted one before, so it could be a total failure. But listen, if you don't want to, I get it."

The corners of his full lips quirk up. "I didn't know you could cook." It's the first break in the ice separating us, and it's so uplifting I can't fight my own smile.

"Listen, Williamson, I'm actually a great cook."

He's silent a moment, and the air around us snaps with something I don't dare call attraction. "What time?"

"Seven?"

"Sure. We'll be there."

I smile again, though I do my best to hide the pure joy I'm feeling since he accepted my invitation. "Great. See you both then. Eloise doesn't have any food allergies, right?"

"Nope." He takes his tools and leaves the duplex without another word, and I stand staring at the door with a wide smile for far longer than I should. I've spent nearly every day over the last week beside him, and this is the most he's spoken.

Is it possible that I'm finally starting to break through the walls between us?

My cell rings, and I'm so focused on Silas that I actually jump. "Hello?" I answer, after checking the screen and seeing Reyna's name on the screen.

"Hey! What are you up to?" Michael's wife questions.

"Silas just finished up the final touches on my roof, and I'm getting ready to start doing some cleanup. I was actually going to call you, though."

"Yeah? What about?"

"Well, I know Michael ended up staying in town and turning down that protective detail so he could be here to help with the storm damage, so I wanted to invite you both over to dinner. I'm inviting the others, too. You just called me first."

She's quiet a moment. "Is Silas going to be there?"

"He helped, so yeah. I invited him."

"Good." I can hear her smile through the phone. "What can I bring?"

"Just yourself."

"You said you had cleaning to do?"

"I did," I reply, nervous at the inquisitive nature of her questions.

"Good. I'll come help. I'm going to pick up Eliza and Andie, too. I'll let Margot know, and she can head over as soon as she's done at the B&B."

"You don't have to do that." Panic claws at my throat. They want explanations. Conversation I've been dodging for the last week.

"Listen, Bianca, you've been avoiding us while you worked on your house. Now it's done, so we're coming. Love you, okay? Bye!" Reyna hangs up the phone, and I stare down at it slowly, trying to figure out why I wanted girlfriends. Isn't this why I avoided having them? So I didn't have to partake in idle conversations about life things I'd rather not discuss?

And over cleaning?

My two least favorite things.

I take a deep breath and survey the dust-covered living room. My replacement couch is currently covered in plastic sheeting, my rug protected by painter's cloth.

I guess help wouldn't be such a bad thing.

And I am trying to be more open, so maybe this won't be so bad?

After pulling up the cloth on the floor, cleaning paint brushes and rollers, and taking the paint cans to the garage, the doorbell rings.

I laugh to myself as I head over and pull open the door. Eliza, Reyna, and Andie are standing on the other side, dressed to clean, wide smiles on their faces.

"For you, dear friend," Reyna offers me a to-go coffee cup.

"Thank you."

"It's the least we could do since Reyna is forcing conversation." Andie winks and steps inside. "Whoa, this looks amazing. Can barely tell that the ceiling caved in last week."

"Silas did good work."

"And speaking of Silas," Reyna starts, setting her purse down.

"We're just going to jump right in, aren't we?" I ask.

"We are. Because I didn't get the full story out of Michael. He gave me a brief overview after I called him out for being grouchy."

I wince. "Sorry. I know I deceived you guys. That's not even the half of it. I brought a threat straight to your door."

"Please." Eliza shakes her head. "You didn't do that. You're not responsible for the actions of others, Bianca."

"I still lied."

"You misled," Andie replies. "But we forgive you for it."

Even though I know I should be cleaning, I take a seat on the plastic-covered couch. The others do the same. Andie and Reyna both sit on the couch alongside me, while Eliza sits on the ottoman directly in front.

"My father was a cruel man," I tell them. "But I didn't see him as one until the day he killed my mother. Up until my seventeenth birthday, I thought he was the greatest man in the world." I shake my head. "Talk about a rude awakening." Because it makes me uncomfortable to be vulnerable, I offer a soft laugh. "I was way wrong about all of it. Anyway. He was a murderer, and I was afraid, so I ran to the only other person I thought could protect me." This is the part that I kept from everyone else, including Silas. The moment I never wanted to share but feel as though I should. "I was engaged to the son of a friend of my father's. Looking back, I should have known. But I didn't think my father was anything more than a murderer. I never would have thought he was behind—well—the drugs, guns…any of it."

"And how could you?" Reyna asks, reaching forward to rest her hand on my leg. "You couldn't have known, Bianca."

"I should have though. Anyway, I went to Yarrow in hopes that he could help me get away. I was terrified. He tried to force himself on me that night, and when I refused, he slapped me." I can still feel the sting of the hit even after all these years.

Eliza gasps.

Andie looks ready to hunt him down.

Reyna is furious.

"I kneed him in the groin, then took off, stealing all the money I could find. I paid someone to erase who I was, and I lived on my own until my eighteenth birthday when I joined the Army. It was by accident that I went in the recruiting office at all, to be honest. I thought I was being followed, and it was the closest building to me. I walked in, and when I walked out I knew my father would never be able to touch me again."

"Oh, Bianca." Eliza reaches forward and squeezes my hand. "I'm so sorry."

I shrug, doing what I can to keep myself together. "I buried that part of me until my father sent someone after me. They grabbed me from base overseas and brought me to Cambodia to help my father. He was in rough shape when I arrived, but I could have saved him. When he started coding, though, I just put my hands up and stepped back. I watched him die." A tear slips from my cheek now. "I watched him die on that table, and I felt no guilt over it."

"He'd murdered your mother," Andie tells me. "Destroyed your life and countless others."

"It wasn't even until then that I knew the true scope of who he was. I'd done my research on him after I ran, watching to see if he'd be pinned for my mother's murder, but what I found was minimal compared to what I learned that day." I try to recall what it felt like to stand there and watch the man who raised me die.

Try to recall if I felt any kind of remorse. But in that moment, I didn't. And doesn't that make me a bit of a monster, too?

"They were going to kill me for his death," I tell them. "But they'd needed River's permission to do so."

"And then Silas came in," Reyna says.

I laugh and wipe a tear away. "And then Silas came in. He looked like an animal," I recall. "His hair wild, his chest bare and streaked with crusted blood, injuries, and dirt. His bare feet were bleeding, I even remember the trail of blood as he came into the room. He had to wrap his feet in gauze before we left that room so they couldn't see which direction we went."

"Silas as a wild animal," Reyna says. "I can see it."

The door opens, and Margot bursts in. "I came as soon as I could. Matty is watching the front desk. What did I miss?" She sets her bag down.

"Bianca has a psychotic father who died due to a medical complication, she was engaged to a man whose butt she kicked when he attacked her, and Silas looked like a wild animal when he came in to rescue her," Andie says.

I laugh, enjoying the light tone she uses. It lessens a bit of my own weight. "When you say it like that."

"I have a way with words," Andie replies with a shrug.

"So, Silas, wild animal." Margot sits beside Eliza on the ottoman. "What happened next?"

"We spent a month together in that jungle. I'd been fighting to keep the infection in two of his injuries localized, but they were stab wounds I later found out were reopened every single day over the course of his captivity. The skin was tattered, and it was a constant struggle to keep him standing. But he was so positive. So happy."

"Silas? Happy? Positive?" Andie looks around the room. "Like, am I the only one who thinks he can be a bit of a grump sometimes?"

I know she's trying to lighten the mood, but comparing him then to who he is now hurts. Because while I recognize losing his sister took a toll, I can't help but feel like I broke him first. "He wasn't like that then," I say. "His mood is the only thing that kept me going when I wanted to just give up. He made me a mud cake for my birthday."

"Really?" Reyna presses a hand to her heart.

"That's so sweet!" Margot exclaims.

"It was. I fell in love with him while we were out there, barely surviving. It was the best birthday I'd had since before my mother died. He made it special by just listening and being there."

"Bianca, that is adorable," Andie says.

"It was," I admit. "Until it wasn't. Not too long after that, we were tracked down by men sent by my uncle, and he found out who I was. I'll never forget the way he looked at me, with such disgust that I could feel the hatred in it. We were rescued by his cousins. They have a company that tracks down lost people, and his sister sent them after us. After we were brought back stateside, we went our separate ways. Both of us needed to return to our command so we could be debriefed."

"And you never saw him again?"

I shake my head at Margot's question. "Not until Lance called and asked for my help after Michael was missing. He knew we'd been friends and that I had a medical background, but I had no idea he knew Silas, too, or that he was the one helping track him through the swamps."

"Oh, man." Andie shakes her head. "That's a lot."

"He still hates me," I tell them.

"No, he doesn't," Eliza replies. "A man who hates you wouldn't do that." She points to the ceiling.

"I lied to him."

"You did, to all of us," Andie agrees. "But I have to agree with Eliza on this one, a man doesn't offer to patch a hole in the ceiling when he hates you."

"I wouldn't even say he's trying to keep his distance," Reyna says. "Maybe he's just trying to find his footing. You guys do work together now, and with a history like that—" She whistles. "It takes a lot of processing."

"Did anything happen between you two out there?" Andie asks.

"He kissed me," I admit. "We were watching the rain fall and talking about our lives before, and we just sort of looked at each other and he leaned in. But it was just a kiss. And the next day, everything fell apart."

Silence surrounds us as the memory of that day settles

in my mind. It had been a soft kiss, a gentle caress of lips and nothing more, yet it stoked a fire in my heart that hasn't gone out since.

"Who knew Silas had this whole romantic side to him," Andie says.

"Had being the key word," I reply with a sad smile as I stand. "I better get this place cleaned up, I still have dinner to make."

"Oh, I almost forgot!" Reyna laughs.

"You guys really don't have to help me."

"Please, we are absolutely helping," Margot says. "We're family. It's what we do for each other."

Tears blur my vision as I nod. Family. I haven't had a family in a long time, and this is the second time in a week that word has been used for me. I can only pray it's not a mistake that I stay.

CHAPTER 9
Silas

"You look contemplative."

I glance over as Pastor Redding takes a seat beside me on the park bench. Eloise is laughing happily as she runs up and down the playground equipment that resembles a pirate ship.

"A bit," I admit. "Just a lot on my mind these days."

"I can understand that." He leans back. "Eloise has grown so much in the time you guys have been here."

"She has," I reply. "What has you out and about?"

"I went and met with Juniper Kline. She's been having some troubles lately and wanted someone to talk to."

While I don't know Juniper well, I do know she's one of Mrs. McGinley's close friends. "I hope everything's okay."

"It will be," he replies with a smile. "How are things with you? I hear you patched Bianca's roof."

"A tree fell through it."

"I'm eternally grateful no one was seriously injured in that storm. It was a rough one, though not as bad as it could have been."

"It was our first hurricane," I tell him, nodding to Eloise. "She was pretty scared for most of it, but as soon as —" I trail off, not wanting to admit it out loud.

"As soon as?" he presses.

"I carried Bianca over and cleaned her leg. Eloise fell asleep on her."

"Aww, that's sweet. Sometimes having someone other than a parental figure around helps. And sometimes it does the opposite. There was a hurricane, oh wow, about two decades ago, that came through here. Terrified my daughter, Kassandra. She refused to sleep until our neighbors came over after their front window broke. They have a daughter about her age, and the two of them just fell right to sleep on the floor." He smiles at the memory. "I remember thinking to myself, how are they sleeping through this chaos?" He laughs. "Kids are resilient."

"That they are," I agree. "Bianca has been reading that Bible you gave her," I blurt. I'm not sure why I say it. I definitely don't want to be talking faith with a pastor, but the words just pour out.

He smiles. "Good. I'm glad she is."

"Yeah. She seems better, now that she's been reading it."

"God's Word will do that," he replies.

"For some."

He turns toward me. "You don't think it would for you?"

"It never has before."

"Never?"

"Not that I've seen," I reply. "And I'm not interested in trying again."

I expect him to push. To pressure me with scripture or tell me that I'm wasting my time not actively reading the Bible and attending church. Instead, Pastor Redding stands and offers me a kind, understanding smile. "You let me know if you ever change your mind on that. I think we could have some things to talk about."

It's ridiculous that I'm this nervous.

But I've changed my shirt three different times in the last ten minutes as I prepare to head over to Bianca's for dinner. I can already hear the people over there, their mumbled voices happy as they visit.

It's a dinner party.

There will be a lot of people over there. So why do I feel like I might be sick to my stomach?

"Uncle Lassy!" Eloise calls out. "Your phone is ringing!"

I head into the kitchen where I left my phone, and check the readout. As soon as I see my cousin's name on the screen, I answer. "Hey, Bradyn."

"Hey, cousin! Good to hear your voice."

"Yours too, what's going on?"

"Not much. We just got back from a job in Ireland."

"Ireland, huh? Exciting."

"Yeah, it was an easy one. Nineteen-year-old ran off and married her high school sweetheart, whom mom and dad did not approve of. They thought she was kidnapped, but turns out they were just on their honeymoon. Happy ending for her, but they're not pleased."

I laugh softly. "Well, glad she ended up being okay."

"Same. How are things in your neck of the woods? Still enjoying Maine?"

"It's nice. Eloise loves the beach."

"We have beaches in Texas, you know."

I snort. "Galveston is no Maine."

He laughs. "Fair enough. We just miss seeing you guys." After I'd adopted Eloise, we spent some time with my cousins on their ranch in North Texas. I'd nearly stayed…but then I got the call from Lance that Michael was missing. Eloise stayed with my uncle and his wife on the ranch, while I'd flown out to help.

And then I'd seen her.

Bianca looked exactly like she did all those years ago, and even though I never want to admit it, she's the reason I moved to Hope Springs. Because I wanted to see her again. I wanted to keep seeing her.

Even if it was at a distance.

"We miss seeing you guys, too. We'll be out for Christmas, though."

"Good. Mom will be happy to hear that." His tone shifts. "How is everything else?"

"Fine," I reply. He knows Bianca is here. That she's right next door. That I'm still struggling with the weight of a past I'd wanted to die with me. And while I didn't tell him who she truly was until she was long gone, he was far more understanding than I would have been if the situation was flipped.

"Silas, I'm here if you need to talk."

"I know. But I'm fine. Things are good. Work is good, though…"

"What?"

"Do you know if River Culvers is still active?"

"I can look into it. Why do you ask?"

"A man turned up dead. Had ties to the Culvers family."

"Do you think they're coming for you?"

"Not me," I reply.

"Bianca. I can look into it, for sure."

"Thanks. We haven't had any other issues show up, and no one else has been lurking around town that we know of, but I can't shake the feeling this wasn't a coincidence."

"You know how I feel about those," Bradyn replies.

"Same as I do. Which means you don't think they happen." I sigh into the phone. "I don't want to lose what we've got here, but I can't risk Eloise."

"We'll get to the bottom of it," he promises. "And you

know you've always got a place here if you ever want to return home."

"Thanks. Talk soon." I end the call and set my phone down, then lean on the counter. I should take Eloise to Texas. Let her stay with my aunt and uncle until we get all this figured out, but until I know there's something *to* figure out, I can't bear to part with her. There haven't been threats to my life or hers, and honestly no active threats toward Bianca either.

And no movement for a week.

The best move here is to stay put until I know more. But the first sign of danger will have us on a plane so I can get her to safety.

"You ready?" I ask her as I grab my keys and phone off the counter.

"Yes! Can I bring my coloring stuff?"

"Sure thing, pack it up."

We're just stepping out onto the porch when Bianca's door opens for Lance and Eliza. I'm standing just out of sight, but close enough to hear Eliza say, "She wants her auntie Bianca." Then hands her daughter, Mable, to Bianca who takes her, a wide smile on her face.

"Her auntie Bianca loves her so much. Yes, she does!" she says, turning in a slow circle.

All of the oxygen seems to disappear from the air around me as I stand here, watching the scene play out in the doorway. Wearing a floral dress, her hair braided down her back, Bianca looks absolutely stunning.

But it's more than that.

It's the joy that encircles her. The happiness practically radiating from her.

Bianca's emerald gaze finds mine as she stops and my stomach twists.

"Hey," I manage.

"Hey," she repeats.

I clear my throat. "Thanks for the invite."

"Are you making s'ghetti?" Eloise pushes into the house.

"I am," Bianca replies with a smile.

My niece beams at her. "That's my favorite!"

"I might have heard something about that." Bianca's gaze finds mine again, and I have to force myself to look away. Thankfully, Lance and Eliza head into the house, so I follow them, doing my best to keep myself from looking at Bianca again.

Space. That's what we need.

"Okay, baby Mable, want to help me stir some sauce?" she asks.

Mable giggles in response, so Bianca heads back into the kitchen.

"Just waiting to burn out, huh?" Lance asks, a knowing grin on his face.

"Yeah. Just waiting to burn out," I reply.

He laughs. "That's what I thought too." He claps me on the back. "Let's get you some water. Looks like you could use a cooldown."

"I HAVE TO SAY, BIANCA, THAT WAS SOME OF THE BEST spaghetti I've ever had," Pastor Redding compliments as he stands and starts collecting plates.

"Thank you. Let me grab those." Bianca gets up and tries to take the plates from him, but he keeps them just out of reach.

"Nope. You cooked, we clean."

"But I really don't mind."

"We do." Kyra stands and collects the rest of the empty plates.

"Uncle Lassy, can I go color now?"

"Sure thing, Nugget. Your bag is on the couch."

She hops down from her chair and heads into the house. She kneels at Bianca's coffee table and starts pulling out the coloring book and crayons she'd insisted on bringing. Just watching her calms the nerves that have been twisting ever since I saw Bianca in that doorway.

I should have insisted on keeping the boundaries I've built in place. But even as I know they should have remained firm, I feel them slipping a bit more each day. Especially over the last week as we worked so closely together.

That voice in my head that keeps telling me it's not her fault who she was born to grows louder and louder each day. It reminds me that she wasn't sure she could trust me and that's why she wasn't honest.

Yet whenever I reach for those voices, hoping to cling to it, another one slips in…and it speaks of betrayal.

"You good?"

I turn toward Lance. "Fine. Why?"

"You just look a bit strained."

As I fully face the table again, I'm surprised to see that it's just him and me sitting down. Even Michael has gotten up and gone in to help the Reddings' with cleanup. And Bianca stands at the edge of her porch beside Eliza who is cradling baby Mable.

The wind picks up a strand of her hair, and she smiles.

It's like a punch to the chest.

"Not strained," I manage. "Just focused."

Lance follows my gaze. "Ahh, I get it."

"No," I insist. "Not on her. I've got a lot going on."

"Sure. I get it."

I start to argue. Start to push back. But then Bianca turns to face me and I find myself captivated by her once more. Bianca has always had a hardened look about her. Pain that she's transformed into armor. But tonight, she looks free of it.

Like a woman unburdened.

Is it truly the Bible that's bringing her so much peace? Or is this an act because she's scared about what might be coming?

Lance's phone dings, pulling my attention away from the dark-haired beauty. "No update. Sheriff Vick still has nothing." He shoves the phone back into his pocket. "Either it was all coincidence—which I'm not buying—or whoever killed him is laying low. Either way, I don't like it."

"Me neither. I asked my cousin Bradyn to look into it. He's got some good intel on the Culvers'."

"Good," Lance replies. "We could use all the help we can get." He sighs. "Bianca said this guy is patient. What do you know about him?"

"Not much," I reply truthfully. "He's Lucian's half-brother, born due to an affair his father had with his secretary."

"Was it a family business?"

"No. Lucian started it using the contacts his father had as a defense attorney. His father died when Lucian was twenty-five, and it's suspected that it was murder. A way to get his dad out of the way so he could grow the organization without fear of being caught."

Lance studies me. "What do you think?"

The man picks up on subtleties most miss. It's what made him a great Ranger, captain, and what makes him good at his job now. "His dad was an abusive drunk and had an affair. I believe he killed him out of revenge after his dad turned over his client list."

"Then that's what we'll go with. When did Lucian bring River into the organization?"

"Right after he killed his father. Before that, River had been living in a halfway house, drunk and addicted to every drug known to man."

"So Lucian cleaned him up and brought him in as number two."

I nod. It's not hard for me to recall what's in that file. I memorized it. And a man like River Culvers, and what he did to my team and me—not things you forget. "I didn't know about Bianca. Lucian kept his family life under wraps, so she was never spotted."

"When did you find out about her?"

"When the enemy tracked us down. They thought it was hilarious that I had no idea who she was." She'd charged out of the brush, ready to fight for both our lives. My chest aches as I recall the terror on her face when they'd forced her to her knees in that jungle, their weapons trained on us both.

But they'd threatened me and she immediately pleaded for my life. Then threatened to take her own if they didn't let her go.

I swallow hard. I'd been so angry at her for lying that I'd nearly blocked that out of my mind.

"What happened next?"

"My cousins showed up and subdued them. Apparently, my sister sent them after me once the U.S. government pronounced me dead. They'd found the bodies of the rest of my team and assumed I was gone, too. But she said she felt I was alive. 'Twintuition' is what she'd called it." Another ache. Because I'd laughed it off when she'd said that, yet I'd known she was dead before the call even came in.

A feeling that I couldn't ignore, like a piece of me was gone.

"So your cousins came after you. And then?"

"Nothing. At the time, I didn't tell them who she was, and she didn't offer the information. I did end up telling them later, but it was after we'd already gone our separate ways to be debriefed."

"Why didn't you tell your cousins who she was?"

I consider his question because it's something I've wondered too. I remember how angry I was. How hurt. Bianca and I had walked through hell together and the entire time she'd been the daughter of a monster.

But then I remember the ferocity on her face when she'd charged out of those trees, ready to die for me. And I realize that even after all this time, my feelings for her had never left. They changed, sure, but I was only masking the love with anger because, somehow, it hurt less than admitting I'd been betrayed by someone who had come to mean everything to me in a short period of time.

"Repayment," I tell him. "She saved my life, and I felt like I owed her one."

Lance studies me because we both know it's not the truth. Thankfully, though, he doesn't call me out on it. Not directly, anyway. "One of these days you're going to wish you'd been honest with her," he says. "About how you feel."

"Maybe," I admit. "But not today."

It's near ten when Eloise finally falls asleep. After eating way too much dessert and having an insane amount of fun with everyone, she'd been bouncing off the walls. It had taken a warm bath, lavender oil in the diffuser in her room, and three bedtime stories before she'd finally started yawning.

After checking to make sure the front door is locked and retrieving the baby monitor from the kitchen counter, I head out onto the balcony that overlooks the ocean. It's a clear night, the stars shining brightly overhead, and the sound of the ocean waves crashing into the rocks has the weight of my stress melting away.

That is, until I glance to my left and see Bianca on her side of the porch, Bible cradled against her chest, eyes closed. At first, I'm captivated by what a beautiful sight she makes in her white sweatshirt and seafoam green leggings, her hair loose around her face.

But then I realize that this level of relaxation is not normal for her. And I can't tell if she's breathing.

I leap over the divider separating us and rush to her side, adrenaline surging through my system.

Did they somehow get her while I was putting Eloise in bed? Was she sitting out here relaxing and—"Bianca?" I run my fingers over her cheek.

Her emerald eyes flutter open at the sound of my voice and she stares up at me, gaze still blurry from sleep.

Touching her feels right. Being near her feels right.

So I pull away and take a deep breath. "Sorry, you fell asleep on the porch."

"What? I—" She sits up straighter, letting the Bible slide into her lap. "I'm sorry. What time is it?"

"Sleeping out here in the open isn't smart."

"I didn't mean to fall asleep. I was reading Proverbs and must have drifted off."

"It's not smart," I repeat, feeling a familiar panic clawing at my chest. What if they're watching, just waiting for a chance to strike?

Her gaze narrows on me. "Like I said, I didn't mean to fall asleep." She yawns, then sets the Bible on the small table beside a mug of what I imagine is now cold tea. "What time is it?" she asks again.

"Ten."

"I haven't been out here long then. I must have been really tired." She makes no move to get up and go inside. "Eloise get to sleep okay?"

"Fine. She was wound up."

Bianca smiles and looks out over the ocean. "Yeah, I imagine she was. Oh, to have that type of energy."

"Are you really feeling better after reading a book?" The words are out of my mouth before I can stop them. They're ruder than I meant, but as a man on the hunt for his own answers, I find the change she's seemingly undergoing intriguing.

"The Bible? Yes."

"Really? They're just words on a paper."

"They're really not," she replies. "I mean, I used to think so too, but now—" She shakes her head. "I see them differently."

"How so?"

"Because for the last week I've been reading the Bible every day, actively praying, and I have found more peace than I've ever had. It's this feeling, this soul-deep warmth that we're not accidents, but created by a God who loves us. Who chose us."

"Created to go through pain. Misery. Loss. Grief. Sickness. You call that loving?"

"I do," she replies without hesitation. "Because even though we face trials here, even though horrible things are carried out by people who are driven by sin, we're not walking through it alone. We don't face any of it by ourselves. And the peace that knowledge brings me is beautiful. I still have questions," she adds when I don't immediately respond. "Things that I need to work though, but I know that I won't be alone."

"Then explain the jungle. Explain what we went through there. Why would God, as loving as you say He is, allow us to suffer like that?"

Bianca stands and closes the distance between us. I start to move, start to take a step back and leap over the barrier separating our two porches, but instead, I remain rooted.

"I don't know the answer to that, but I believe there's a bigger purpose. A reason we went through what we did. And maybe it was as simple as bringing the two of us together."

"We both know Lance. That would have brought us together."

She reaches up and rests her slender hand on my chest. I stiffen beneath her touch, feeling both rooted and absolutely terrified. She's always had that effect on me though

—the ability to shut down every single thought and fear with a simple touch. "But you didn't know Lance until you were in the hospital after being rescued. If you hadn't been in that jungle, or if you'd died with your team, you would never have met him, and our paths never would have crossed. Now, I imagine you would've been okay with that, but I'm glad we met." She smiles and withdraws her hand.

I wish she was still touching me.

Wish that I had the words to tell her that I would not have been okay with that. Because meeting her in that jungle was the only thing that made me want to keep living after I'd lost my team.

CHAPTER 10
Bianca

Church dismisses on Sunday morning with a hopeful song from the worship band, and I stand to gather my things with a smile. Eliza does the same beside me, though she's grabbing a diaper bag and not her purse.

"You're sure you're okay with this?" she asks Lance for what is probably the dozenth time.

"Yes, baby, go. Have fun. Bring me a burger."

"But—" She glances back at me, then him again. "You're sure. She's been fussy. What if—"

He smiles and leans in to kiss her nose. "My love. I can handle our daughter—fussy or not—for a few hours. Go and have a fun lunch."

"Okay. But call me if she won't eat her bottle or go down for a nap."

"I will, honey. I love you," Lance kisses her and she

slings the diaper bag over his shoulder as he lifts the infant car seat with their smiling daughter strapped in.

"I love you, too. And I love you, my little sweetie." She leans in and kisses Mable's nose.

"Ready?" I ask as she turns to me.

"I am, I—wait. Is that Silas?"

I turn, certain that it can't be. But then I see him with Eloise, standing in the back wearing slacks and a crisp white button-down, talking to Pastor Redding. "He came to church?" Our conversation last night comes rushing back.

Is Silas looking for answers, too? Peace?

Tears blur my vision as emotion surges through my system. And then his gaze finds mine. I can't look away. Can't bring myself to break the connection we seem to share despite the fact that, at one point, both of us wished didn't exist.

Eloise tugs on his shirt and he looks down at her, so I tear my gaze from him and wipe my eyes quickly. By the time I turn back to Eliza, she's grinning at me and Lance is already gone.

"What?"

"I think I just found our topic for lunch," she replies with a laugh and loops her arm through mine.

"What are you talking about?" We make our way toward the door.

"You know what I'm talking about."

The sun is warm on my face as we step out of the church. The salty sea air filling my lungs is something I will never tire of, and I let Eliza guide me toward the cross-walk so we can head to the diner. My mind is reeling, thoughts on Silas in church.

All of a sudden, the hairs on the back of my neck stand on end. I stop walking, immediately reaching to draw the firearm holstered beneath the waistband of my skirt as my gaze scans the rooftops.

And then I see it.

The smallest glint of light.

"Get down!" I scream and throw myself in front of Eliza.

Searing pain shoots through my right arm, but I don't let it slow me down as I sprint behind her, covering her back until we're behind the cover of a parked car. People in front of the church scream and race back inside for safety.

Another bullet.

This one pierces the sidewalk right where I'd been standing a mere heartbeat before.

Thankfully, the bullet hit my non-dominant arm, so I draw my weapon and aim it over the hood of the car.

I scan the rooftops again and see a man running away, a rifle bag on his shoulder. "Stay here," I order and kick off my heels, then dash across the street. My heart is racing, adrenaline surging through my system and numbing the pain in my arm.

Warmth drips down to my wrist, so I know I'm bleeding, and the asphalt is rough against my bare feet, but the only thing I can think of is getting to the shooter before he can hurt anyone. I reach the building seconds after he's dropped down from the fire escape.

"Freeze!" I yell, but he doesn't stop.

I fire.

He grunts as the bullet hits its mark, tearing through the flesh of his leg, but he keeps moving, albeit slower than before.

I sprint toward him as he disappears from sight. By the time I get behind the building, he's gone. And then tires screech against the pavement. I leap to the side, barely managing not to get hit as a vehicle speeds past me and out of view.

"No!"

"Bianca!" Silas is at my side.

"He got away. No plates. Dark sedan." I'm all business, quickly reciting the information I have so I don't forget it.

"You've been shot!" He yanks the button-down shirt from his torso, ripping the buttons as he wraps my arm with the once-clean fabric. "What were you thinking?"

"That I needed to stop him." I continue staring down the path he took. How far could he have gone with a bullet wound like that? Will he go to the hospital?

"Alone?"

"I was the only one on the street. Did you see him? I didn't get a good look with the mask he was wearing. We need to get to the hospitals, see if he checks in—"

"Bianca." Silas grips my face, cradling it in his hands and forcing me to look at him. His eyes are wide and wild, his cheeks red.

"What?" I ask. "We need to get Lance. The others. We need to—"

"Get you to the hospital," he interrupts. "You've been shot. Do you hear me? You're losing a lot of blood."

For the first time, I look down at the blood covering my skirt and pooling on the pavement beneath me. It's a lot. Enough that it's already saturated the shirt he wrapped around my arm.

It means the bullet likely caught my brachial artery. Which also means that if I don't get help, I'm going to go into shock.

Soon.

As if on cue, my vision wavers. Dark spots invade my sightline.

"I think I need to sit down. Just for a minute."

"No." Silas catches me as I start to fall. "Call an ambulance!"

I HATE HOSPITALS.

Everything about them. The smell. The feeling. The chill that seems to hang in the air. As twisted as it sounds, I prefer field medic tents to big hospitals like this. Probably because that's what I'm used to.

The hospital in Hope Springs isn't even that large, but it feels like a hospital and that's enough for me. Which is why I'm endlessly grateful that I'm already at home after Doc removed the bullet that tore through the artery in my arm and stitched me back together.

Sheriff Vick managed to catch the shooter—he'd driven off the road after passing out due to blood loss. So, go me, I guess.

The pain in my arm is extensive since I refused anything stronger than over-the-counter pain meds once the surgery was done, but I can manage. Unfortunately, it's not the worst pain I've faced. At least I have a sling this time.

Lance assured me that he'd call when they had anything, but I check my phone again just in case. I'm desperate to face down with the shooter myself, but he'd made me come home for the night, promising that I could be in the interrogation room as soon as I got some rest.

But rest is the last thing I need.

There's a knock on my door, so I cross over and check the peephole. Silas stands just outside, his hands in his pockets.

I haven't seen him since I passed out.

He didn't come to the hospital, not that I blame him. He probably hates them more than I do. But I'd hated that he wasn't there.

I open the door, and his gaze levels on me. "How do you feel?"

"Fine. Do you want to come in?"

"Sure."

The kettle I'd been prepping in the kitchen beeps,

signaling the water is ready, so I leave him to shut the door and head into the kitchen. "Do you want some tea?"

"No."

"Okay." I pour water into the mug with my bag of tea. "Where's Eloise?"

"Staying with Michael and Reyna. I figured it was safer to have her away from here until we figure out what's going on. I might end up taking her to Texas. So she can spend some time with my cousins."

I swallow hard, hating the idea of them leaving. "Makes sense."

"I'm sticking around, though," he says. "Staying here so I'm close if something happens."

"You should leave, too, Silas. You're all she has." I turn to face him, surprised to find him closer than I thought he'd be, with only a foot between us. I suck in a breath, the intensity in his green gaze captivating my thoughts.

"You could have died," he says softly.

"He nearly got Eliza because she was walking beside me."

"You could have pushed her to the side, taking you both out of the path of the bullet, but instead you threw your body over hers."

He's not mad, or at least that's not the impression I'm getting. But is it too much to hope for worry? That he really does care for me and my life?

"She has a baby. I didn't think about my life. Only hers."

"Like when we were in the jungle?" he asks.

I stiffen. "What?"

"You charged out of that brush without a single thought for your own safety."

The memory is branded in my mind. The terror as I heard them slam Silas to the ground, telling him to speak his last words.

I had fully processed what would happen if I intervened. And I'd done it anyway. "They would have killed you."

His gaze drops to my lips, then locks on mine again. "And you were going to stop them."

"I wasn't planning to save you," I admit. "I knew we were both going to die, but I didn't want to lose you and survive."

Silas stiffens, his muscles going rigid. I worry that I've said too much. That he's going to turn away from me for good, now that he knows my act of heroics was actually one of cowardice. The fact is, I couldn't face life knowing Silas Williamson was no longer breathing.

He'd come to mean so much to me in that month we were running for our lives. We'd laughed together despite our fear, clung to happiness even though we knew the likelihood of us walking away was basically nonexistent.

"I should have told you who I was," I say. "Should have mentioned it the moment you came to me. But to be honest, I wasn't entirely sure you were real. I was dehydrated and exhausted."

"You should have told me," he says. "But I should have

at least tried to understand why you felt like you couldn't."

"I did trust you, Silas. It was never about that."

"Then what was it? Because for years, I've tried to rationalize why you didn't ever tell me. Did you think I would leave you to die? Turn you over in exchange for my own freedom?"

"No, of course not."

"Then what, Bianca? Because even though we didn't know each other long, I thought we'd gotten close. Even if the affection we felt for each other was manufactured by the fact that we could have died at any moment, I thought we'd at least end up friends."

"We were more than friends," I insist. "I just—"

"What?" he demands again, tone turning frustrated.

"I didn't want you to look at me like you looked when you talked about him." I open my eyes and a tear slips free. I wipe it away quickly. "Every time you spoke about Lucian and about what you'd have done to him if given the chance, you looked so—I don't even know a word appropriate for the level of fury on your face. And rightfully so, but I didn't want to become an enemy. I couldn't stand the thought of you seeing me as one."

He studies me, the frustration on his face fading away. "I wouldn't have seen you as an enemy."

"You would have," I reply. "Because it's how you've been looking at me ever since I showed up in Hope Springs."

CHAPTER 11
Silas

I should have stayed next door. At least there, the lines were drawn. But standing here in her kitchen, so close I can breathe in the scent of her ocean-pine shampoo, I can't think straight.

An enemy?

Is that how I've been thinking of her?

"You're not my enemy."

"No?" she asks, then wipes a tear away. I long to reach forward and erase the pain from her heart. "You could have fooled me."

"Lucian slaughtered my team. Those men were my friends. My brothers. He killed them in front of me, discarded their bodies like trash, then River spent a month torturing me. I bled. Over and over again. My bones broken. My soul practically ripped from my chest and thrown to the side like garbage right alongside my will to live."

"I know."

"No," I reply. "You don't. When that man came and freed me, I thought I was either hallucinating, or it was another trick of theirs. A way to taunt me with freedom only to rip it away at the last second. And every time I took a step forward, I wondered if it might be my last." I move a bit closer, and Bianca tips her beautiful face to look up at me. "And then I heard you." The words are spoken so softly they might as well be a whisper. "I heard a voice say *save her*, and I knew I couldn't leave you behind."

Even though there's a warning screeching in my head, even though I know it might be a mistake, I reach out and touch her face.

Gently. Just a whisper of contact.

But she closes her eyes and her lips part. I have to fight the urge to lean in and taste the lips I've been dreaming about. The woman I've been in love with for over a decade.

"With the first look at your face, I couldn't help but wonder if you were some kind of angel in captivity. You were too beautiful for a place like that. Too beautiful to have blood splattered on your clothes, your face bruised."

She snorts. "I was never an angel."

"I know that now," I reply as I drop my hand and take a step back to put some distance between us. "But I let you in. And I don't let people in."

Realization hits her, and her expression falters. "I'm sorry, Silas. If I could take it back, I would."

"I haven't been able to get you out of my head since

that day, no matter how hard I tried. I locked myself in a cabin in the middle of the woods in Montana, but even that wasn't far enough to outrun the ghost of you. I'd been determined to die out there in that cabin, until my sister had her accident and I was made sole guardian of Eloise."

Bianca's walls haven't gone up once during this conversation, which is yet another first. Normally, her cheeks are red, her eyes hard and lacking all emotion as she buries anything that makes her feel.

But she's open now, hearing my words.

"Sorry doesn't cut it," she says. "But I wish I would have told you. Even if it meant you hated me from the moment we met, or you left me to die in that jungle. I wish I would have been honest, Silas."

"I want to feel the peace you're feeling right now. I want to find a way to let go of the anger I still carry. For my sister, my team, my brother-in-law, you—" It's been so long since I spoke this much. Since I unloaded any kind of —anything, really.

"I was at their funeral."

"What?" The words catch me off guard. "Who's funeral?"

She swallows hard as though she's afraid to continue. "Your sister and brother-in-law's. I stayed in the back, as out of sight as I could be, but I wanted to be there even though I knew you wouldn't want me there."

Her confession forms a pit in my stomach as I recall one of the worst days of my life. Since our parents passed shortly after we'd graduated high school, and we'd never known any of our grandparents, it had just been Sierra and me.

The two of us against the world.

Then she'd met her husband while I was on my first tour, and the three of us grew close despite me trying to keep my distance so they could flourish as a couple.

The day I buried her, part of me died. And I know, without a doubt, had I not been standing there holding Eloise as they lowered my sister's body into the ground, I might have just jumped into the grave right alongside her.

Losing her felt like losing a vital piece of myself, and I haven't been the same since.

I try to recall seeing Bianca or anyone who looked like her, but I'd been so overwhelmed with grief I doubt I would have recognized anyone, least of all someone I was earnestly trying to forget.

"How did you know?" I ask. "That she was gone?"

"You weren't the only one who couldn't forget the other." Bianca crosses her arms, the closest she's come to putting up those walls, though her eyes remain clear. Soft. "I couldn't let you go, either. You were constantly on my mind, and one day I had the urge to look in on you, so I did an internet search and saw an article on the accident. I know how much Sierra meant to you. How much you loved her, and that you had no one else. The thought of you suffering through that alone was too much for me, so I booked a flight to Texas."

I'm not a man of many words by choice, but right now, even if I wanted to, I have no idea what I would say. The fact that she was there, that in the pain of losing my sister, Bianca showed up.

Bianca continues, "You were wearing a dark suit, your face clean-shaven. You looked so broken." A tear slips down her cheek. "Eloise was in a black dress, but you'd given her a bright yellow flower to hold. I remember it being such a happy color. A splash of life amidst death."

"A yellow tulip," I recall. "I'd picked it outside of their house so she could take it with her."

She smiles. "I was going to say something. Talk to you. But when I saw you with Eloise, for a moment, I thought—"

"She was mine?"

Bianca nods, tears glistening in her eyes. "I thought that maybe you'd found someone else and moved on, and the last thing I wanted to do was be a reminder of the nightmare we suffered through. Not when you may have found some sliver of happiness."

I open my mouth to respond—with what, I'm not sure —but right as I'm about to start speaking, a shrill cell tone slices through the air. Bianca reaches onto the countertop behind her and checks the readout, then answers.

"What's up?" Her gaze locks with mine. "We'll be right there."

<hr>

AFTER BATTLING WITH MYSELF OVER THE NEED TO BE CLOSE TO Bianca and the desire to shove her away, I drive the both of us over to the hospital, where the shooter was currently recovering.

Was being the key word there because, according to Lance, he's now dead despite being expected to make a full recovery.

Lance and Jaxson are both waiting for us at the entrance.

"Jaxson, good to see you back," Bianca says as she embraces him.

I try not to be jealous. After all, Jaxson is happily married to Michael's sister, Margot, but seeing Bianca wrap her arms around another man makes my stomach churn. I want it to be me. I've always wanted it to be me.

"Glad you've come back," I say, offering my hand.

"When Lance told me Bianca was shot and we had a potential crime war on our doorstep, I knew I needed to come back."

"You shouldn't have left because of me," Bianca insists. "You've had a lot going on yourself."

After being estranged from his father for most of his life, they reconnected when his father showed up to apologize after receiving a terminal diagnosis. He passed almost two months ago, and Jaxson has been in California ever since.

"Things were wrapped up," Jaxson replies. "I was ready to come home. How's the arm?"

"I'm managing."

"Glad he missed."

Bianca smiles. "Same."

"So, what happened?" I ask, desperately needing a change in subject.

"We're not sure yet. Doc says it could have been a blood clot, but we won't know until the autopsy comes back. Personally, I'm betting on foul play. I think somehow, someone got to him. Elijah is with Sheriff Vick running down the names of everyone who had access to his room."

That's where I'd place my bet, too. If I were a gambling man, that is.

"You said you found something strange in his room?" Bianca questions. Her skin is a bit pale, and she'd been silent the entire drive over, her thoughts elsewhere. I wanted to ask if they were on me and what might have been, or on the man who was yet another loose end to be tied up.

"Yeah. Let's go take a look. I asked Sheriff Vick to wait to bag it until you saw it. It's untouched right now, and while I know it could be nothing, I can't shake the feeling that it's—well—you'll see."

A deputy's stationed outside the door, and he offers us a nod as we move into the room. Bianca stops in the doorway, her gaze traveling around the space. I do the same, scanning for something that feels out of—

"Oh no." Bianca turns white as a sheet, her eyes going wide as she narrows in on a stuffed teddy bear sitting on the windowsill.

It's worn, and honestly, I might have thought it was just something the nurses put in the rooms to make patients feel better.

"The bear?" I ask, my gaze traveling to Jaxson and Lance as though either of them can answer me.

"I—" She crosses toward it, gaze locked on it like it's a magnet drawing her in and she's helpless to its pull.

"Bianca, what is it?"

She reaches out with trembling fingers and lifts the bear. As soon as she removes it, a folded-up sheet of paper is revealed.

With her gaze locked on the stuffed animal, I reach for the paper and unfold it.

Selena Culvers, you and one guest are formally invited to a dinner party held at the Boston Harbor Hotel tomorrow at seven p.m. This will be a black-tie affair, and no weapons will be allowed through the door.

This is a peaceful invitation.

A white flag, if you will. Consider your now-deceased shooter a gift, showing you that I mean you no harm.

If you ignore me, then things will escalate. Something I assure you I have no time for and you truly do not want. Tell your SEAL I said hello.

Your uncle, River

Fury burns in my veins, and I have to actively fight the urge to crumple the paper in my hands. My gaze lands on the name at the top. *Selena Culvers.* I raise my gaze to Bianca, who is still studying the bear. "Selena."

Her gaze flies to mine, eyes wide. "What did you say?"

I ignore her, gesturing to the bear. "Your uncle left that for you."

She nods. "It was mine. When I was little. My mother

gave it to me. I had to leave it behind when I ran. I never thought I'd see it again." She wipes the tears from her cheeks and offers it to Lance. "Can you have Elijah check for any recording devices?"

"Done." He takes the bear. "What does the note say?"

"It seems Bianca's uncle wants to catch up over dinner. He also confessed to this murder." I hold the note out for her to see, and both Lance and Jaxson flank her to get a better look.

"Selena. No one has called me that in nearly two decades."

"That's your name?" Jaxson asks.

She nods. "This doesn't make any sense, though." Bianca hands the note to Lance. "He takes out the man he clearly hired to kill me, then offers me a white-flag dinner party?"

"The murder is likely punishment for failing," Jaxson offers.

"This dinner invitation is clearly a trap," Lance adds.

"His threat isn't subtle, though," Bianca says. "And he will carry through. Today was just the beginning."

Lance's jaw hardens. He nearly lost his wife today. I imagine he's a lot angrier than he's showing right now. "We can head to Boston and do some recon at the hotel."

"If my uncle senses anyone sniffing around, he's bound to react," she tells him. "And I can promise you he already knows everyone who works with us." She walks to the window and looks out. "He's playing with me. It's all a game to him. 'Come see the wealth that could have been yours.'" Furious, she turns to face us. "And if I don't go, he's going to wreak havoc on everyone here."

"And if you do go, he's going to kill you." I consider his sign-off. *Tell your SEAL I said hello.*

"My guess is he's coming for you, too," Jaxson says after rereading the note. "He calls you out right here."

"This can't continue," I say, feeling the choking fingers of fear gripping my throat.

"You don't have to be involved," Bianca says. "Take Eloise, leave town for a while. You said you could go back home, right?"

"And what?" I demand. "Leave you here to die?" Even as Eloise's safety is my top priority, and I told myself I'd put the both of us on a plane at the first sign of trouble, the idea of leaving Bianca here to fend for herself against someone we both know is capable of evil is unthinkable.

"I'm not going to die. We'll find a way to catch him, and then you can come back."

"I'm not leaving, Bianca. I had face-to-face interactions with River. I know him—well. Possibly better than you do. There's no way I'm leaving everyone I care about behind so I can run and hide."

"What about Eloise?" she demands, cheeks reddening. "She has to be your top priority."

"She *is* my top priority," I snap. "But that doesn't mean I have to run and hide. I can keep Eloise safe and stand my ground. I came to Hope Springs for a fresh start for both Eloise and me. I wanted safety. Security. Both of which are not possible while River walks free. You and I both know that he's caught my scent. If I run, he'll track me down as soon as he's finished with you." I'm not entirely sure that's correct, but I know River to be vengeful. I recall his ferocity when he drove a blade into my shoulder because I'd shot him when my team was first attacked.

He doesn't let things go, and he's incredibly patient.

Bianca's gaze is dark, her glare furious. She wants me to leave. But why? Is it truly about Eloise's safety? Or is it me she wants gone?

The thought creeps into my mind, pushing out all others.

I raise my gaze to Lance. "I'm not leaving."

"I'm not asking you to," he replies. "As far as I'm concerned, we need everyone on this." His phone buzzes, and he lifts it and checks the readout. "Elijah's got something. We need to get to the office."

CHAPTER 12
Bianca

Exhaustion pulls at my body, making my eyes heavy. Every step sends fresh pain shooting through my arm, slicing up through my shoulder and into my neck.

It's been a day.

A dead body.

A missing killer.

And now a trap masquerading as a dinner invitation.

I have to go. Even though it's a trap, and I really don't want to see my uncle, I know that ignoring him isn't an option. The threat he made has remained at the front of my mind since I first read the words, and I've no doubt he'll make good on it.

Bodies will start piling up, and the last thing I ever want is to be the cause of someone else's pain. I'd rather hand my life over than have him hurt anyone in retaliation.

My thoughts drift back to Silas. I wish he and Eloise would leave. Somewhere they can be safe. Maybe that cabin in the mountains Silas was talking about. Or his cousin's ranch. Anywhere there will be some distance between them and whatever River is trying to bring raining down on us.

The image of him standing before me in that hospital room, furious at the mere idea of leaving…I can't help but wonder what the motivation is. Unfinished business between him and River? A thirst for vengeance? Or could it be that he's worried about me?

"There's no way I'm leaving everyone I care about behind so I can run and hide."

Everyone I care about.

I can't help myself. Even though there's danger hanging over me like a thick, suffocating blanket, I smile.

"That's a happy smile."

I shoot up off the couch and draw my weapon, aiming it down the hall with my good hand. A man, cloaked in shadows, slips out of the dark hallway. His face is aged, his hair gray, but I'd recognize him anywhere. "River," I growl.

"Little Selena. It's good to see you all grown up." He smiles and steps further into the living room. I eye the cell phone on the coffee table. "I wouldn't. I've got a gunman on your precious SEAL at the moment, and he's more than happy to pull the trigger should anything happen to me."

Because I can't take that risk, I lower my weapon, though I keep it gripped firmly in my hand. *Lord, please be with me now. Please grant me strength to face this nightmare and walk away. Please protect Silas and Eloise, and any others River may be threatening. In Jesus' name I pray. Amen.* "What do you want? I got your letter."

"Good, good." He runs his fingers over the counter. "Sorry about the gunshot."

"Sure you are."

"If it helps, he was supposed to miss. He was just supposed to scare you. You were never in any real danger."

"And how about everyone on the street?" I ask. "They could have been hit."

He shrugs and takes a seat in the armchair to the left of the couch. "Collateral damage."

"I don't believe in innocents being caught in gunfire."

"No, you never had the taste for games, did you?"

"Not when those games involve someone's life."

He gestures toward the couch. "Sit with me, will you?" I don't move. River rolls his eyes. "You're making me nervous, Selena, and I don't think that will make the man listening to us very happy. It might make his trigger finger a bit shaky…"

Slowly, I lower to the couch, though I keep my weapon in hand.

"Good girl." He grins. "So, how are you? It's been a long time."

"Seems like you know since you've been stalking me for years."

"You always figured it out rather quickly," he says curiously. "But this time you knew you were being followed, yet you didn't run. Why is that, I wonder?"

I don't answer. This is the thing about River. He *loves* playing games, like a predator toying with their prey.

"I suppose it has something to do with that SEAL and his little girl."

I try to keep my expression flat. Try not to let him see that the very thought of him watching Silas and Eloise makes me want to vomit.

"Oh, don't worry, Selena. I have no intention of hurting him or the girl." He laughs. "Well, at least not the child."

"Why are you here?"

"Family gathering," he replies.

"Funny. Everyone else is dead."

River's expression falters a moment, the cool mask he wears so elegantly falling. Anger replaces it, and for a moment I worry that I've gone too far. After all, if he's telling the truth, one word from him would end Silas's life.

"You'd better watch what you say. I don't often let murderers live. Yet I've allowed you to walk this earth for quite some time even knowing you were guilty."

"You have no say over whether I live or die," I reply.

He arches a brow. "Found God, have we?"

"Yes."

River throws his head back and laughs. "I think the small town is getting to you, Selena. Anyway. I won't take up too much of your time. I just wanted to pop in, check on things, and make sure you knew better than to ignore my invitation."

"You did have me shot earlier today. I might not feel like attending a dinner party."

River stands and crosses over toward me. He takes a seat on the couch and leans in, the stench of his cologne filling my lungs. My stomach churns. "You will go," he replies, pushing some of my hair behind my ear. He leans in and whispers, "Or I will burn this entire town to the ground with everyone trapped inside." His expression turns amused as he stands. "See you at dinner, Selena. Wear something your mother would have worn. Classy. And bring that SEAL with you. I'd love to visit with him again, too."

The mention of my mother is a sucker punch.

"Stay there for three minutes. After that, you can get up. But a second sooner, and"—he holds up his cell phone, showing that the call is still active—"*bang*." He turns and heads back down the hallway, and I remain where I am.

The seconds might as well have been hours. I don't even dare reach for my cell phone, terrified that he'll see that as a move against him. Tears burn in the corners of my eyes as the adrenaline wanes, making way for the shock of what just happened.

I sat face-to-face with River Culvers.

My father's brother.

The man who has been trying to kill me.

Who promised to do so the last time we saw each other.

The same man who tortured Silas for a month and hunted us like wild animals when we were in the jungle.

Yet I'm still breathing. Which begs the question…what does he want from me?

"I SHOULD HAVE BEEN HERE," SILAS ALL BUT GROWLS. "Should have stayed put."

I'd made the call to Silas first, desperate to make sure he was okay. Then I'd called Lance so he could alert the team to River's presence in Hope Springs. Silas arrived right after I got off the phone with Lance, insisting on clearing both sides of the duplex to make sure everything was locked down tight.

Lance, Michael, Jaxson, and Elijah showed up shortly after, now that Caleb is working for Knight Security and handling video monitoring tonight.

"No. He only came because you were gone." That much, I'm sure.

"How did he get in?" Lance questions.

"Her bedroom window," Silas replies. "Broke the lock and came through. The system was unarmed," he adds with a glare at me.

"I checked the house when I got here," I tell them. "So it had to have been while I was in the shower."

Silas snarls something under his breath, then turns away and puts both hands on his hips. He's furious with himself, which is absolutely ridiculous. I can take care of myself, something I've proven time and time again.

"He is expecting both Silas and me at that dinner tomorrow."

Silas whirls. "What?"

"He mentioned you specifically," I reply. "Though I'm not sure why he wants either of us there. Something has to be happening. Something big."

"We can't move on him without proper cause," Lance warns.

"Agreed." Jaxson crosses his arms. "Guy like him will be lawyered up to the teeth."

"Then Silas and I can go in and gather evidence."

All eyes turn to me.

"Look, he may be at a hotel, but I can almost guarantee something big is going down at that dinner. If Silas and I can get proof that he's dirty, then we can stop him."

"Do you really think he's just going to let you both walk in and out of there?" Elijah demands. "There's no telling if you'll come out alive."

"He threatened the *entire* town, Elijah. A threat he's more than capable of making good on. I can't risk it."

"Neither can I," Silas replies.

"This feels like a mistake." Lance rubs both hands over his eyes.

"We're up against a wall," I remind them. "He has the power, and he knows it. He knows we know it."

"How are you going to defend yourselves?" Jaxson asks. "He said no weapons, and we're not James Bond. There are no lipstick lasers in our arsenal."

"That's a thought though," Elijah comments.

Lance shakes his head. "You can't even fight right now, Bianca. Not in your current state." He gestures to my injured arm.

"I'll make it work," I tell them. "Besides, I'll have a SEAL with me," I reply, glancing at Silas.

The corner of his lips twitch.

"He said no weapons," Lance says again. "So, we make do with no weapons. Elijah, can you get us set up with some undetectable coms?"

"Already done," he replies. "They're currently at the office. Crisp. Clear. And they won't be picked up by any detectors."

Lance nods in appreciation. "Good. Then we'll use those to stay in touch, and the rest of our team will be ready to go in should things get heated. Caleb can watch the monitors, and I'll call in Alex to help him out if any client issues arise, which means we'll practically be all boots on the ground."

"We can't alert the police. There's no telling if some of them are on his payroll," I say quickly. "No one can know, or this goes even more sour than it already is."

"Agreed." Lance stands. "Do you want to stay at the lighthouse tonight?" he asks me. "Caleb is on monitors so you'll be protected."

"Yes," Silas says. "She should."

"No." I look to him, annoyed that he spoke for me. "If River wanted me dead, I'd be dead. If he wanted to abduct me, he would've. Nothing will happen tonight."

"He could have just been toying with you," Silas snaps.

"No. He wasn't. Now, I was shot earlier today, my arm feels like it's going to fall off, and I'm tired. I would really like to get some sleep."

"I'm staying on the couch." Silas slips out of his jacket.

"No. Silas. Seriously. You're right next door, I don't need you on the couch."

"Seems like we've overstayed our welcome," Elijah quips, then heads for the door. "I set up temp cameras on every entry point of your house, and Caleb is monitoring them!" he calls out, then leaves before I can respond.

"What? Cameras?" I ask Lance.

He shrugs. "You're one of our people, Bianca, and we protect our people. Goodnight." With a smile, he leaves, trailing Jaxson out the door.

Men.

"You are not sleeping on my couch," I tell Silas.

"Yes. I am." He lays down, propping an arm beneath his head.

Irritated and knowing I've lost, I head into my room, retrieving a blanket and spare pillow from my closet, then step out and throw them at him. He grunts, giving me a bit of satisfaction as I make my way back into my bedroom, then shut and lock the door.

The truth is, I feel better knowing he's down the hall. But letting him know that, or even fully admitting it to myself, feels like a dangerous mistake.

CHAPTER 13
Silas

"Be good for Lance and Eliza, okay, Nugget?"

"Okay." Eloise squeezes my neck. "I love you, Uncle Lassy!"

My throat tightens as I fight back every bit of fear and sadness as I say goodbye to the single most important person in the world to me. "I love you, too, Nugget. You be good and have fun, okay?"

"Okay!" She straightens, then skips away and takes a seat at the table to work on the coloring book Eliza bought her.

"We're going to be just fine," Lance's wife assures me. Eliza's gaze is soft, and she reaches out to gently squeeze my arm.

"Just keep her safe." My throat constricts, tears threatening to fall. What if this is the last time I see Eloise?

"With my life," Eliza says. "I promise you, Eloise will be safe with us."

"I know she will be." Because if I'd had any doubts, we'd be on the first flight out of this place and somewhere River and his organization couldn't find us. "We'll be back later tonight, but I'll be by to get her first thing in the morning if that's okay."

"Totally fine." Eliza smiles. "She's a doll, and I know Mable loves having her around, too." She glances over her shoulder at the infant currently enamored with the mobile hanging over her swing.

I can't tear my gaze away from my niece. I could die tonight. That realization hit home at about two this morning while I was lying on Bianca's couch, staring up at the ceiling fan above my head. Reaching into my back pocket, I withdraw the rolled-up manila envelope I'd brought just in case, and hand it over to Eliza.

"This is all of Eloise's information. Her birth certificate, insurance card, social security card, and a will that names you and Lance as her legal guardians should anything happen to me."

Eliza's eyes fill as Lance puts his hand on her shoulder, his expression hardening. Up to this point, he's been standing silently beside his wife.

"I needed to make sure the bases were covered. Just in case. The will was made up a few months ago when I moved here. I do have family in Texas, I'd like you to still take her to visit them from time to time, but my cousins travel a lot and my aunt and uncle are up there in age."

"Silas—" Eliza steps forward and wraps her arms

around me. "You're going to be just fine." She steps back. "But we are honored that you chose us."

"You're the best people I know," I reply. "And I know that you'll treat Eloise as your own should anything go wrong."

"We will," Lance says. "But it won't."

"It might. And I needed to make sure I'm ready for it just in case it does." My gaze lands on Eloise once more. *Please don't let this be the last time I see her.* It's not a prayer… exactly…but the words come into my mind and I send them out anyway.

Lance's phone beeps, so he withdraws it and checks the readout. "Time to go, Bianca is ready and they're pulling up any minute." He kisses Eliza. "I love you. Be careful tonight."

"We'll be just fine," she replies. "Andie, Reyna, Margot, Matty, Lilly, and Alex are coming over for dinner and games. We'll be safe."

I know they called Alex, the diner owner and a former Army Sergeant, so he could be here with everyone just in case River decides to strike out while the rest of us are occupied. Sheriff Vick is on high alert, too, everyone standing by just in case this is all one big distraction.

My guess is he wants nothing to do with this town or anyone who will be staying behind though. His fight is with Bianca and me. And it's been a long time coming.

With one final look at Eloise as she laughs at something on the television, I make my way out of the house and down the front steps. A black limousine is parked out front, compliments of Michael, who's acting as our driver tonight.

The door opens, and I lose the ability to think straight.

Bianca is stunning in an emerald gown the same shade as her eyes. Her dark hair is curled and loosely braided back, leaving her elegant neck on full display. She's swapped out her tan sling for a black one that matches the elbow-length black gloves adorning both hands.

She's done something smoky with her eyes, and her lips are painted a deep red.

Gorgeous.

She's absolutely gorgeous.

"We'll be behind you most of the way," Lance tells me, then gets into a black SUV parked behind us, Jaxson at the wheel.

"You clean up nice, Williamson," she says as she scoots over so I can climb in.

I take my seat across the inside from her, trying to put some distance between us now that the interior feels beyond stifling.

"How is Eloise handling the sleepovers?"

"Fine."

"How are you handling the sleepovers?"

I glare at her. "Can we focus on what the plan is tonight?"

"Sure. No personal talk. Got it." She looks annoyed, though. "We go in and keep an eye out for anything that might prove what River and the entire organization is up to in Boston. If we can get enough proof, we can shove him in a cell and throw away the key."

"Weapons? What if there's a fight?"

"I have a nail file in my purse. If they let me keep it, that's the closest thing I have."

Given her arm is in a sling, the bulk of the fight will be on my shoulders. I'm responsible for not just my life, but hers as well. *Who am I kidding, I would have considered myself responsible even if she hadn't been shot yesterday.*

The weight of tonight is crushing, and I lean back to close my eyes, hoping to alleviate even a bit of the pressure. The last time I was face-to-face with River Culvers, he was driving a dagger into my shoulder.

A sharp blade that had been heated so it cauterized as he ripped it out. And it wasn't the first time.

"'Therefore put on the full armor of God, so that when the day of evil comes, you may be able to stand your ground, and after you have done everything, to stand,'" Bianca says.

I open my eyes, surprised to find her reading from the open Bible on her lap.

"'Stand firm then, with the belt of truth buckled around your waist, with the breastplate of righteousness in place, and with your feet fitted with the readiness that comes from the gospel of peace. In addition to all this, take up the shield of faith, with which you can extinguish all the flaming arrows of the evil one. Take the helmet of salvation and the sword of the Spirit, which is the word of God.' I'm sorry, I needed it, and I thought you might, too."

The words she read aloud settle in my mind with a warmth I hadn't expected to feel. "Feel free to keep reading," I reply.

She smiles, and a vise tightens around my heart.

And as she continues reading aloud, saying words that I've never heard before, I realize just how desperately I'm craving the same peace she seems to have found.

THE DRIVE TO BOSTON TAKES HOURS, BUT IN MY MIND, IT'S mere minutes. I've managed to talk myself out of making Michael turn the limo around at least three times, but I remind myself that whether we go or remain in Hope Springs, River's still coming for us.

The difference is, at least if we're here, he has no reason to be there.

"We're here," Michael calls back.

Bianca's pale complexion shows just how afraid she is, but as she bows her head, I'm fascinated to watch a total calm settle over her. Color returns to her cheeks, and when she opens her eyes and raises her head, she looks like a woman ready for battle.

Her emerald expression lands on mine. "You ready for this?"

"No," I reply. "But let's do it anyway."

Michael climbs out and opens the door, then offers us a brief nod as I hand him a twenty I'd brought with me. A tip to keep up appearances. He closes the door behind us, and I offer Bianca my arm. She slips her uninjured arm into mine, then takes a deep breath.

We start walking, heading into the hotel lobby where a man dressed like a butler awaits. "Miss Culvers and Mr. Williamson?" he asks.

"Yes," Bianca replies, stiffening beside me.

"Right this way." The man doesn't show any expression, just turns and begins walking down the hall toward the elevators. He presses the call button. As we wait, I check the surroundings.

Armed men at both ends of the hallway.

Likely more outside the hotel.

So much for no weapons.

Bianca leans her head against my shoulder. "I see them," she whispers.

I don't respond.

The elevator arrives and we climb on. The man who'd greeted us scans a white plastic badge against a reader inside, and the doors close. Confined, I start to feel a familiar panic. I hate small spaces.

They all feel like cages. Bianca leans against me again, and I know she's trying to soothe my fear. So even as I desire to keep at least some walls up between us, I rest my head against the top of hers, breathing in the feminine scent of her shampoo.

It eases my frayed nerves and helps me recenter.

Then the doors open, and elegant orchestra music fills my ears. The aroma of food drifts toward us, filling my lungs and making my stomach churn. Food is the absolute last thing on my mind as we step off the elevator and into a ballroom that has been decorated with one long table, a dance floor, and an orchestra.

Guests mingle, most of them men and women I don't recognize.

Until I see him. River Culvers stands just a few yards from us, dressed in a tuxedo, laughing alongside a smiling woman.

Every muscle in my body goes rigid, and my desire to rip him apart where he stands nearly obliterates all rational thought.

"We're in," Bianca says softly. I know it's more for the team's benefit than mine, but it grounds me.

"Good. Stick to the plan. Alert us of any changes," Lance says.

River's gaze finds mine and he smiles, an animalistic grin that's branded in my nightmares for so long, I can no longer recall a time he didn't haunt me.

"You okay?" Bianca asks, looking up at me.

I grunt, unsure I can trust what might come out of my mouth should I choose to speak at this moment.

River excuses himself and crosses toward us, the woman no longer on his arm. "Selena and Silas. What a beautiful couple you make."

"No need to check us for weapons?" Bianca asks.

"You're far too smart to bring one in here after I explicitly told you not to. But not to worry, should one appear at any point this evening, I have an entire team of people on standby just outside of your sleepy little coastal town." His words are murderous, but his tone remains pleasant. *Sadistic man.*

"You hurt anyone, and you'll suffer greatly," Bianca tells him with a smile.

River's own spreads. "I doubt that very much." He turns to me. Standing about six inches shorter than me, he has to tilt his head to look up at me. "How have you been, Silas? I have to admit, I've missed our little chats."

I growl.

His amusement is plain as day. "There's the murderous SEAL I remember. How's fatherhood treating you? Real shame about your sister."

I lunge forward, but Bianca pulls me back. "Are we here so you can taunt Silas? Or is there a purpose to this? Because I can assure you, in a fight with no weapons, you still don't stand a chance."

River's gaze doesn't leave mine. "Last I remember, I did."

"You had me chained," I growl. "Let's see if the outcome is the same while I'm free."

River laughs. "You always amused me. More so now, though, I have to say." He leans in. "You've never been free, Silas. I merely loosened the leash." He turns to Bianca. "We'll get to the reason soon enough. For now, though, I expect you to be pleasant to my guests, dance at least once, then join us for dinner. Once everyone is excused, we'll move onto the business portion of this meeting."

"Dance? You expect us to dance?" she asks.

River looks at her, then at me and grins. "I do. Both of you."

"You do realize I just got shot, right?"

He looks annoyed. "You have one good arm. Make it work."

"Why?"

"Because this is a party, Selena, and you need to act as such." He looks past us and nods. "Excuse me for a moment." Moving away from us, he heads over to greet a couple who just came in.

"This is—I don't even know what this is," she mutters.

"Sounds to me like you two should hit the dance floor," Michael quips through the earpiece.

My stomach churns. I'm a good dancer. Great even, thanks to the lessons my mother forced me to take when I was young. But the idea of holding Bianca close, of breathing in her scent and feeling her body move with mine—how am I supposed to keep my head with her so near?

Is that his point? Does River somehow know what she means to me and he's using her to distract me?

"Shall we?"

"It seems we have no choice," I all but growl.

"Don't be so grumpy," Michael says. "Could be worse."

"Aren't you supposed to be silent?" I ask quietly.

Michael chuckles. "It's okay to make the most out of a situation, Williamson."

I guide Bianca over to the dance floor and she snakes her good arm up over my neck. Given I can't hold her other hand, I keep both on her waist and we begin to move slowly to the music.

She moves in closer, leaning her head against my chest so she can keep her gaze on River without seeming suspicious. I close my eyes, taking just a moment to appreciate the way she feels against me. The way we fit.

How many nights did I dream of her?

There were moments I craved running for my life, because I'd been blissfully unaware of who she was, and focused on doing just what Michael said—making the most out of a bad situation.

When did I stop doing that? When did I stop being so positive?

Because even after everything I'd suffered through, I'd retreated, sure, but I'd still been relatively positive about life.

And then Sierra's death changed everything.

I take a deep breath.

"You okay?" she asks, pulling away to look up at me. I'm captivated by the golden flecks in her emerald eyes, and the way the light makes the green of her dress shimmer.

Despite the danger we're in, the risk if this plan goes sideways, I find myself relaxing just slightly here in her presence. Because with Bianca in my arms, the darkness surrounding us feels a bit lighter.

"I am," I reply, sincerely hoping it stays that way.

CHAPTER 14

Bianca

River hasn't left the ballroom the entire time we've been here. He's talked to nearly everyone in attendance, laughing and sharing drinks as though he's not a monster masquerading as a man. I can see through the charming smile, though, to the evil man beneath.

Silas and I have been all over the dance floor, trying to get close enough to him to overhear something that could be of use—all while trying to ignore the energy buzzing between us. Not that I know whether or not he's feeling it too. I just can't imagine I'd be this affected if he's not in the slightest.

The feel of his arms around me is something I'll never forget.

"Dinner time!" an announcer calls out.

The music stops.

Silas keeps his arm on me as servers pull out the dining

room chairs in unison. It's almost creepy, the way they move as a singular unit, prepping the spots for everyone. Together, we watch as the guests take their seats, laughing happily as they do so.

Do these people know what River is? Or are they all playing their part?

"Miss Selena Culvers!" the announcer calls out. "Here." He holds out a chair directly to River's left at the head of the table. I look to Silas, who maintains his hold on my arm for a moment.

"Mr. Silas Williamson!" another announcer calls, then pulls out the chair across from mine, directly to River's right.

"Come, sit," River orders as he gestures toward the chairs. "We're all waiting on you."

I turn around, scanning the room for anyone else who might still be standing, only to find that we're the only ones who haven't taken their seats. When did that happen?

Slowly, Silas guides me over toward my chair, then helps me sit and growls at the server behind me. The man pales slightly, then backs away and lets Silas push my chair in. Then, with eyes on River, he walks around the table and sits directly across from me.

You could hear a pin drop as everyone watches.

"Great. Now. Let's eat!" River holds out both hands and the servers leave the room, only to return moments later with individual silver trays for everyone.

Names are engraved on the top in elegant script, making me painstakingly aware of the fact that River has meticulously planned out and given orders for each person's meal. This can only mean one thing. Someone's going to die tonight. The question is…who?

Neither Silas nor I touch our food as the others around the table—River included—remove the silver lids to their trays. Only two people at the table hesitate. And it's that hesitation that catches River's eye.

A trick I only know because it's one straight out of my father's book. I saw him use it one time…the night he killed my mother.

My free hand tightens in my lap.

"Here, let me help you." River removes the lid, then picks up my steak knife and a fork.

Silas's hand closes around the handle of his own blade as he watches while River cuts up the steak on my plate—humming the entire time. Once it's in tiny pieces, he sets the knife down right in front of me, leaving the fork on my plate.

Is he mocking me? Daring me to take it?

Silas lowers his hand back into his lap, but the knife is no longer on the table. My heart begins to pound, and I lock eyes with him. Surely, he's not going to attack River at the table.

"So, Silas how *is* fatherhood?" River asks, then shoves a piece of steak into his mouth.

Silas doesn't answer.

"You were always so chatty before, now you have nothing to say?"

Still, Silas doesn't speak.

"How about you, Selena? How are things in your life?"

"At the moment? Not great."

River laughs. "How's the arm?"

"It hurts."

"So little conversation, wouldn't you say so, James?" He shifts his attention to the man sitting to Silas's right.

"Not nearly as chatty as I remember them."

Even if I didn't understand what he was as I was growing up, I learned two things while living under my father's roof.

One, if you open your mouth, you'd better have something powerful to say.

And two, never let them see you're shaken.

So, I turn to James. "Funny, I don't remember you at all."

His gaze hardens. "You wouldn't. But your mother would."

The anger hits me so swiftly, I have to force myself to take a deep breath or risk losing the temper I've worked so hard to restrain.

The elevator doors ding.

"Sorry I'm late."

My heart begins to race.

My stomach churns.

Because I'd know that voice anywhere. Dark hair. Tall. Brown eyes. Small scar at the corner of his mouth. Yarrow Bridges is the last man I ever wanted to see again. Even less so than the murderous uncle sitting beside me.

He'd been my closest friend, once upon a time.

Until he'd tried to take what I wasn't freely giving, and I kicked him so hard in the groin he vomited all over the dress I'd been wearing.

He also happens to be the man my father was trying to marry me off to on my eighteenth birthday. The son of a respected business ally my father wanted familial ties with. I'd realized too late that I was a pawn to be used in his twisted game of power.

And it was even later that I realized Yarrow was just like him.

"Darling, it's been too long." He leans down and kisses the top of my head, then takes a seat beside me.

I don't look at him. I can barely breathe thanks to the anger singing in my veins.

Looking to Silas, I try to assure myself that it's all going to be fine. Because I'm not seventeen anymore. I'm not alone in a room. I'm here, in public, with Silas, whose gaze is locked on Yarrow.

"How rude of me. Silas, this is Yarrow Bridges, Selena's fiancé."

The ferocity of Silas's glare is something I've only ever seen one other time—when he'd discovered who I truly was. Then, we'd been in a jungle, dressed in the tattered remains of our clothing. We'd been starving, exhausted, dirty.

Now we're dressed to impress, food right in front of us, yet his look is still the same.

Disgusted at my betrayal.

"No," I snap. "He's not."

"Darling, why must you always be so stubborn?" Yarrow snakes an arm around my shoulders.

Silas leans in. "If you want to keep that arm attached to your body, I strongly suggest removing it from her vicinity."

Yarrow's grin spreads. "This is the infamous Silas Williamson then? The formidable Navy SEAL who managed to somehow escape being chained up in a locked room?"

"It is," my uncle replies. "I told you he's impressive."

"I don't see it." Yarrow keeps his arm around my shoulders.

Silas starts to scoot back, but River clicks his tongue. "Stay right where you are, Silas. There's no violence here. Remember our deal?"

"You didn't make that deal with me," Silas snaps.

"Easy, Silas," Lance says through the coms. "Keep a level head."

"I made that deal with Bianca on your behalf. Any violence here and I'll send a team right into that little town of yours."

We might as well be trapped in a cage, but the look I give Silas promises freedom if he only remains calm. We will find a way out of this.

Please, Lord, let us make it out of this.

CHAPTER 15

Silas

Dinner passes with the speed of molasses in a Montana winter. All around me, guests at the table talk happily, discussing everything from sports to the financial market, but I can hardly hear them. I might as well be underwater for how well I'm paying attention to anything—anyone—except Bianca.

Red ebbs at the corners of my vision as I stare at the man introduced as Bianca's fiancé. He's a predator, that much is clear just from the way he's eyeing Bianca as she sits beside him, her body rigid.

She's staring straight down at her plate, and I imagine she's working just as hard to keep her head as I am. Truth is, I want to rip him out of that chair and throw him from the balcony. *Remain calm.* The words echo in my head, bouncing back and forth and somehow managing to ease a bit of my nerves.

Finally, River stands and announces, "Thank you all for

coming to my lovely dinner party. I look forward to seeing you all again soon. Javier, can you please wait for me in the office?" He gestures to a door off to the right.

"Sure thing, boss. Any particular reason?" the man seated at the end of the table asks.

River smiles, but I see no humor in it. Does the man he called Javier see the same threat that I do? Likely not. "Not at all, I have something I wish to discuss with you. An opportunity I think you'll really appreciate."

Javier grins like he just won a prize. But by the body language River is sending off, that prize is a one-way ticket to the grave. "Great." He turns and leaves, and River waves at his other guests as they vacate the suite, piling onto the elevator in two separate groups.

Soon, it's just River, Yarrow, Bianca, and me.

Woohoo.

"One word and we'll come in," Michael says through the earpiece.

"You're not alone in there," Elijah adds.

"Are we finally to the part where you're going to explain what all of this is about?" I demand.

River looks over my shoulder toward the guard stationed at the elevator. He nods once, and my hand grips the knife in my lap.

Suddenly pain shoots through my head as a loud screeching noise comes from the earpiece tucked away in my ear. It takes me by surprise, but I try to remain calm. Breathing through the pain.

Bianca, though, cries out in surprise.

"Go ahead and remove that thing, darling, it's not going to stop until you do."

She rips it from her ear and sets it on the table.

River looks at me. "I know you have one, too, SEAL. Go ahead and take it out."

"Why don't you come take it out for me?" I growl.

River's expression turns amused. "You really are a hard man, aren't you? I thought having a daughter might soften you up." He snaps his fingers, and I lunge to my feet. But I'm not quite fast enough. Two large men grip my shoulders and slam me back down into the chair.

"No!" Bianca yells. "Get your hands off of him!"

Yarrow yanks her back down into her chair as thug one sticks his fingers into my ear and rips the earpiece out.

He tosses it on the table and the men release me.

"I remember you used to like doing things the hard way before too. Some things never change, huh?"

"Why are we here?" Bianca snaps.

River stands. "We'll get to that. But since I imagine that team that was waiting downstairs will be up here soon, we'll be leaving."

"We're not going anywhere with you," I snarl.

"I'm afraid you really have no choice."

Without hesitation, Yarrow yanks a syringe out of his pocket and drives it down into Bianca's neck.

"No!" I lunge up, but the two men behind me slam me back down into the chair.

Her gaze locks on mine, and I'm forced to watch as she

slips away, her eyes rolling back in her head, her face falling slack.

"She better survive," I growl. "Or there's nothing that will save you."

"Oh, SEAL, if only I were afraid of you. Now, pick her up, and let's get going."

Yarrow lifts Bianca into his arms, and a low growl leaves my chest. "I'll carry her."

"And how do I know you won't run?" River demands.

"Because she can't run with me and I can't move as fast with her in my arms. Now you'll let me carry her, or you might as well drug me, too."

"Absolutely not," Yarrow snaps.

"Give her to him," River orders after taking a moment to consider.

"What? No."

"We're all trying to be friends here, Yarrow. If he wants to carry Bianca's dead weight around, then let him."

I cross over toward Yarrow, keeping my gaze locked on him, my expression furious. "Go on then, Yarrow, listen to your puppet master."

Yarrow stands perfectly still as I take Bianca from him. I can see the shallow rise and fall of her chest, but her complexion is far paler than it should be. *I promise I'll get us out of here.*

"This way," River says as he moves past us, walking through the main door. As we're passing, the office door where he'd sent the man he'd called Javier opens. Two of the guards leave, one of them carrying a black body bag over his shoulder.

"So you didn't even have the guts to look him in the eyes when you killed him," I sneer.

"I see no need for the show of power anymore," River replies flatly.

With Yarrow behind me, I can't turn and run. Can't sprint toward the exit. And I don't trust them not to kill us if I try and stall. So, even though I understand the weight of it, I make my way down the hall and out a back exit into an emergency stairwell.

Good. Hope burns through me. Lance will have had the stairwell covered, which means—but instead of going down, we head up. I listen, hoping to hear the cavalry arriving, but the stairwell is silent.

Completely and eerily quiet.

Where is Lance? Michael? Elijah? Jaxson?

Why are they not here?

We emerge onto the rooftop where two guards are waiting for us. Yarrow reaches out for Bianca. "Give her to me so we can get you ready," he deadpans.

I don't budge.

"Better listen to him, SEAL. I don't think even you could manage to hold onto her while climbing a rope ladder into a helicopter."

As he says it, the unmistakable whirring of blades fills my ears. I look up just in time to see a helicopter hovering above us. A rope cord is dropped, and River is outfitted with a vest that the guard clips carabiners to. Seconds later, he's pulled up into the helicopter.

One of the guards outfits me with a vest and from above, a thick cord of rope is dropped. He clips the carabiners into my vest, then Yarrow hands me Bianca who has a similar vest on her body.

He clips Bianca to my chest as I cradle her close.

Two more ropes are dropped, and Yarrow and both guards clip their vests to the thick cords. Then, Yarrow looks up at the helicopter and makes a sign with his hands.

Air rushes over me as we're drawn upward.

We're mere seconds from the helicopter when the door bursts open and Lance rushes out, flanked by Elijah, Jaxson, Michael, and three uniformed officers.

"Shoot it down!" I bellow.

But I know Lance won't. Because doing so would mean Bianca and I both go down with it.

He lowers his weapon, and all of my hope vanishes. Once this helicopter is out of view, we're at River's mercy. He has the connections to take us anywhere…the ability to disappear.

Is he going to kill us?

Torture us?

Both?

"Close call there. Your buddies move faster than I planned." River fills a syringe with medicine as soon as Yarrow has unclipped me and Bianca and our vests are removed. He holds it out. "Now, you can inject yourself with this and take a little nap, or I'll throw Selena out of this helicopter. Your choice."

"Why not just do it yourself?" I snap, glaring at him.

River leans in. "Because I want you to willingly take it. I want you to be so afraid to lose Bianca that you'll give up every bit of power you have." His use of her chosen name is a game. He is trying to elicit additional emotion out of me. Little does he know I don't care what her name is.

Selena. Bianca. It doesn't matter because it's the woman I can't live without—not the name.

I glare back at him. It's unlikely he wants Bianca dead, but do I really want to call his bluff? "You wouldn't have brought her here just to kill her."

"I would if she's not really the one I wanted." River looks at Yarrow, who slides the helicopter door open and rips Bianca away from me.

Without hesitating another moment, I yank the syringe from River and jab it into my arm. The medication burns as it shoots into my vein. But Yarrow closes the door and sets Bianca back beside me.

"Good boy. Maybe you do have some brains after all."

I don't give him the satisfaction of a response. Mainly because I'm not entirely sure I can speak when I can barely keep my eyes open. I lean back and tug Bianca into my lap, holding her close as I close my eyes.

My last rational thought is of Eloise, and how desperately I'd wanted to watch her grow up.

CHAPTER 16
Bianca

S ilas is still unconscious.

I'm not sure how long ago I came to, waking on a cot exactly like the one he's currently sleeping on. At least the distance isn't too far given the cells are about the size of a large bathroom stall. I'd been able to stretch far enough that I could reach through and feel his faint pulse.

In the time I've been awake, I've checked every single bar of my cell. I've searched for a way out, for a loose spot, for anything that might mean freedom for us. Unfortunately, this place is locked down. Not that I would expect anything else from River. The man is nothing if not consistent.

There's nothing in either cell that can be used as any kind of weapon. We're utterly defenseless. Though, in a pinch, I suppose the bucket they gave us that's supposed to double as a toilet might come in handy. Can't imagine one would be doing much fighting after taking a literal bucket of human waste to the face.

I pocket that thought for later, focusing on all the reasons I have to panic.

Aside from being held captive who knows where, there's the fact that I'm no longer wearing the green gown I'd been in. Someone changed me into shorts and a T-shirt that must have been pilfered from my dresser when River had been in my house. Which, of course, is not nearly as upsetting as knowing someone changed me.

Silas, too. He's in jeans and a black T-shirt, his suit nowhere to be seen.

A throaty groan sounds behind me, so I whirl and rush across, gripping the bars between us. Silas sits up, a bit wobbly at first, then he rubs his head and looks around the cell. He pales.

"You're not alone," I tell him, stepping into his line of sight. "I'm here."

His breathing turns ragged and he sucks in breath after breath, his hands tightening on the edge of the cot.

"Easy, Silas." I reach through the bars, stretching as far as I can, so I can touch him, but it's only enough to brush my fingers across the white knuckles of his hand. "You're not alone," I repeat, then start to draw my hand back. If he's in the middle of a PTSD attack, touching him could make it worse.

But before I can fully get my hand through the bars, he reaches out and grips mine, then gets to his knees in front of the barrier. Fingers wrapping around my hand, he holds on to me but still doesn't say a thing. His head remains hung low, and I tighten my grip, hoping it will help ground him.

Silas spent a month in a cell being tortured by River. I cannot even imagine what he's feeling right now. The panic he must be experiencing, being right back in one, and once again at River's mercy.

On impulse, I reach out with my other hand and, ignoring the pain of my still injured arm, manage to caress the side of his face. Silas leans into my touch, and his breathing begins to slow.

Then, what feels like hours later but is likely only minutes, Silas withdraws his hand and sits back. "Thank you."

"You're welcome." I take a seat on my cot directly across from him. "I don't know where we are, but I'm pretty sure we're not in Boston anymore."

"They drugged us," Silas replies. "And flew us out on a helicopter."

"You were awake for that part?"

He turns his head to look at me. "I carried you."

Knowing that even though I was unconscious, Silas carried and protected me, means more than I can say. "We're going to get out of this. Just like last time."

Silas doesn't look certain.

"God is going to bring us through this."

"Then why let us get taken in the first place?" he snaps, cheeks turning red. "Eloise is going to think I abandoned her. Who knows if I'll ever see her again." Silas stands and begins to pace, looking for weapons or any way to break free.

But I tried every bar.

There are none that are loose enough to break free. The prison is solid. The wall to our back is made of brick. We need to wait until someone comes down here to take us out of the cells. As soon as they do, we can make our escape.

Or die trying.

A door scrapes open, and footsteps echo down the hall. I move to the bars closest to Silas's side, refusing to retreat to the back of the cell as my uncle and Yarrow come into view.

"Well, well, finally awake. Have a nice nap?"

"Where are we?" I demand.

"You'll find out soon enough." Yarrow tosses a pair of handcuffs into my cell, then turns to Silas. "Stick your hands through the bars so she can put those on, big boy," he orders Silas.

"Why don't you come in and put them on me?" Silas holds up his wrists.

Yarrow grins at him, a carnal smile, and for a second I wonder if he plans to take Silas up on the challenge. But apparently, he's a lot smarter than he used to be because instead of opening the cell, he crosses his arms. "Nah, I'd rather not."

"Put them on," River warns. "It won't be like that forever, but until I've fully explained everything, you'll wear them."

I bend over and pick up the handcuffs, then turn to Silas. He still hasn't moved, his wrists out, though his gaze is on me.

"I'm sorry I got you into this."

He doesn't respond, just crosses over and holds his wrists out so I can reach them through the bars. Even as I bind his hands together, he remains silent. I rub my thumbs over the insides of his wrists, hoping the contact will soothe what I imagine is the start of another panic attack. His only response is the slight flaring of his nostrils as he takes a deep, steadying breath.

I step away and turn toward them. "We good now?"

"Sure thing, sweetheart." Yarrow winks and opens the door to my cage, then moves around to Silas's. We step out at the same time, and I rush forward to walk beside Silas as we head toward the exit, though I do allow him to exit first and follow behind. Something I wish I hadn't done as soon as Yarrow falls into step behind me. "You grew up good, Selena."

"Bianca," I snap.

"Excuse me?"

Stopping, I whirl on him. "Selena died a long time ago. You'll call me Bianca."

"No, I don't think I will, *Selena*."

"Stop, you two," River says. "Names are not exactly a priority right now. If she wants to be called Bianca, just do it."

I turn toward my uncle. Why is he taking my side? What game is he playing at?

"Fine, boss." Yarrow leans in. "But Selena will still be my favorite."

My blood ices as my stomach churns. The last time we were this close, he thought he was going to take what I did not freely offer. Does he remember that he threatened to kill me as he laid on the floor, writhing in pain?

"This way." River starts up some steps, ascending to the next floor. Silas pauses at the bottom of the stairs and nods for me to go ahead. I do without hesitation, grateful for the distance between Yarrow and myself.

Yarrow chuckles. "Fine, big boy. Nice and protective, aren't we?"

We hit the top of the stairs and sunlight momentarily hurts my eyes since they're adjusted to the dim light of the basement. But a few seconds and some rapid blinking later, and I see that we're standing in a large, gleaming fully stocked kitchen. Terra cotta tile covers the floor, and the countertops are made of thick pale granite with flecks of gold and copper veins.

There is a woman standing at the stove wearing a long dress, a black apron over the front of it. She pays us no mind as we move through her space and out into an open dining room. River gestures toward two chairs on the right side of the table. "Please, have a seat."

Silas pulls out my chair, and I sit, then he takes a seat beside me as Yarrow sits across from us and River takes the seat at the head of the table—at my right side.

Before I even have the chance to ask where we are, two women dressed in black and white dresses similar to those you'd see maids wearing in old movies come in with two plates. They set one in front of me and one in front of Silas, then rush away to retrieve the others.

"Where—"

"Not yet," River interrupts. "Patience, Bianca." His choosing to call me Bianca is a game, of that I'm sure, but it does still give me an illusion of control, something I'm quite grateful for at this particular moment.

The women return and place a plate in front of River and one in front of Yarrow, while the woman who'd been in front of the stove comes in with four mugs of coffee. She sets one in front of each of us, then the waitress pours steaming hot liquid into them before all of the women vacate the room.

"Good. Now we may talk."

I bow my head. *Lord, thank you for this food and for keeping us alive. Please continue to watch over us and guide us so that we may safely return home. Amen.* When I raise my head, everyone is looking at me.

"I didn't take you for a praying woman," River says. "If that is what you were just doing."

"You don't know me at all." I pluck a berry from the plate and slip it into my mouth. The flavor is beyond appreciated, given the hunger burning a hole in my stomach.

"Well then, I do hope to change that."

"I wouldn't count on it," I reply. "Because I don't plan to be here long enough for that to happen."

River chuckles. "Dear, you will be here as long as I

deem necessary." His gaze turns serious. "Now. Onto business. You're here because I need the services of both of you."

"Services?" My thoughts drift back to the last time this organization needed my 'services.' I'd let their leader die—something I'm fairly certain I would do again.

"You're a spectacular doctor, niece, and I find myself in need of someone to help innocent people who are struggling with health complications and injuries."

"Innocent people?" I snort. "I very much doubt they're innocent if they're associated with you."

River grins. "You don't know me either, Bianca, so do us both a favor and don't pretend you do."

"And what about me?" Silas questions. "What services do you think I can offer you? I'm not a doctor."

"No, but you work private security," River replies. "And it just so happens that Bianca here is going to need a bodyguard."

"I thought these people were innocent?"

"Some of them are," he replies. "Others are less appreciative of what I offer them here and would just as soon take you out to get to me."

"So you want me to play the part of bodyguard? You have men for that, why choose me?"

"Two reasons. One, because you want her alive and safe," River replies. "My men are more volatile, and I need Bianca to survive long enough to do her job."

"And two?" Silas asks.

"Your presence is motivation to Bianca. She either cooperates, or you pay the price."

Dread nearly drowns me where I stand. "Then what? You're just going to let us go?"

"I am," River replies. "As soon as I'm finished here, I'll return you both to that tiny coastal town you seem to love so much."

"And our people there? Are you still lurking outside waiting to burn the place to the ground?"

River shakes his head. "I pulled my men last night. Your town is safe so long as you do exactly what it is I'm asking."

"Let me get this straight." Silas leans back in his chair, his gaze hard. "You want Bianca to play doctor and me to keep her alive while she does it."

"That's correct." River crosses his arms.

"And how long is this supposed to last?"

River looks to Yarrow.

"Projections show us being wrapped up here within two months."

"Two months?" I nearly choke on the words. "We can't be here for two months! We have lives. Jobs."

"It's better than missing the rest of yours by being six feet under, wouldn't you say?" Yarrow demands.

"You can't honestly expect us to be away for two months." I look at Silas, who looks about ready to burn this entire place to the ground with us inside.

"I expect you to do what is asked of you. If you don't, and you let me down in any way, we'll take our frustrations out on those you care about in that little town of yours. One at a time." River looks from me to Silas, then back to me. "And there's more." He takes a bite of his bacon, then drinks some of his coffee.

"More than forcing us to walk away from our lives for two months?" I think of little Eloise, of how confusing it will be for the small child when her uncle—the only guardian she's ever known—doesn't come home.

Of Lance, who will be missing two of his people—his friends.

Michael.

Jaxson.

Elijah.

Our team is alone and vulnerable. I can only hope that since they overheard River's threats at the dinner, they've taken precautions.

"You planning to elaborate?" I snap. "Or do I need to read your mind?"

River glances at Yarrow. "Would you like to do the honors?" he asks.

"Absolutely." Yarrow leans forward and rests both hands on the table. "Selena Culvers, should the day come when I refer to you as such, you will be playing the part of doting fiancée."

CHAPTER 17
Silas

"Absolutely not," Bianca snaps.

Fury sings through my blood, singeing my very soul as it passes through me.

"You don't have a choice." Yarrow leans back.

Bianca turns to River. "You cannot honestly expect me to pretend to be his fiancée."

"Not all the time," he says. "Just in the event that Yarrow's father, Herman, visits. In that case, I'm afraid you don't have a choice. Yarrow's father is an important investor in our little organization, and he's made it well known that he wants the prearranged marriage between you and his son to take place in order to cement our agreement."

"Then find another Culvers."

"There isn't one. You're it."

"Then you better find someone to stand in for me and

pretend to be your long-lost niece, because there is absolutely *no* way I will pretend to be anything to him."

Yarrow stands. "I thought you might say that." He walks around the table, and I track every move he makes, even as I know exactly where he's headed.

There's only one thing in this room that can make Bianca do as he asks.

The cool barrel of his pistol presses against my temple and Bianca's eyes turn molten. "I'll kill your boyfriend here. Maybe that will change your mind."

"You need him," she says. "You both said you do."

"We can find someone else. Maybe I can step up as your bodyguard. I'd love nothing more than to spend every waking moment with you, *Selena*."

Bianca turns to River. "Are you insane?"

To his credit, he looks a bit frustrated at this current turn of events. "Yarrow is right. I need you to play along, Bianca, or I risk losing everything I've built. Everything your father built."

"I thought Bianca made it clear she didn't care about anything Lucian built when she let him die," I quip.

"Shut your mouth." The barrel digs further into the side of my head. It hurts, but there's no way I'll let him see my pain.

"Lower your weapon." Bianca sighs. "I'll do it, but there are conditions."

"Of course there are. I wouldn't expect anything else than negotiation from a Culvers." River glances past me at

Yarrow. "Drop the gun and sit down. Your temper tantrum is over."

Yarrow pulls away, then moves back around the table to sit across from me.

"What a good lap dog you are," I growl.

Yarrow glares at me but doesn't say anything else.

"What are your conditions?" River questions.

"I will *not* be alone with Yarrow. Silas stays with me at all times, and you'll allow us one untraceable phone call."

"One phone call? What is this, prison?" he jokes.

"That's exactly what it is," Bianca replies. "And you'll let us tell those who care about us that we're alive."

River considers, and I find myself seriously hoping he agrees. One phone call is all I need to bring everything and everyone I know raining down on this place like ash after a volcanic eruption. "Fine. One phone call. Silas gets to make it."

"Agreed." She turns to me. "You can tell Eloise hi for me, too."

River reaches into his pocket and withdraws a cell phone, then tosses it onto the table. "The number is untraceable. You get one try. If whoever you're calling doesn't pick up, you don't get a second chance. And if you so much as breathe a word of what you're doing or where you think you are, I'll put a bullet in the both of you and start looking for a new doctor. Got it?"

I don't answer, just reach for the phone and dial Knight Security's number. Since it's public, I don't feel like River having it in his call log is dangerous. The last thing I'll do is dial anyone's personal number.

"Knight Security, this is Caleb."

"It's Silas. I need to talk to Lance."

"Silas?" He sounds relieved. "Here he is."

"Silas. Where are you?" Lance demands.

"I can't tell you that, and I can't tell you why we're gone. I only have one minute, so I need you to give Eloise a kiss for me. Ask her to be extra kind to Bravo." I can only hope he remembers who Bravo is, otherwise, there's no hope of us being found.

"I'll do that. And I'll make sure Bravo is taken care of."

Relief surges through my system, but I do my best not to let it show. "Tell her I love her and that I'll be home soon."

"I will. Bianca?"

"She's okay, too. She's with me, and we'll both be home soon."

"Yes," he replies. "You will be."

"Minute is up." River reaches out his hand.

"I have to go. Keep her safe." I end the call, then hand the phone over to River.

"Who's Bravo?" he asks.

"A dog."

"Interesting name for a dog."

"I was military once upon a time, it seemed like a fitting name."

He doesn't respond, just sticks the phone into his

pocket. "Shall we finish breakfast so I can show you both where you'll be working?"

THE COMPOUND RIVER HAS MANAGED TO BUILD IS RELATIVELY extensive, though I'm discovering everything but the main house is made of shipping containers. They're arranged in two long rows, almost like a manufactured main street.

Emaciated children sit outside in the dirt, the younger ones playing while the older kids watch carefully. I see no men or women, no adults at all, aside from us and the armed guards walking back and forth.

I stop walking.

"What are you doing?" River asks.

"What is this place?" My tone is deadly.

River looks around. Realization must dawn on him because he shakes his head. "You may think me a monster, SEAL, but I assure you I wouldn't harm children."

"You sure about that?" Bianca snaps. "Because they look pretty sick from where I'm sitting."

"Hungry?" he asks. "Sure, but not harmed."

"Hunger is harming them."

"That's on their parents. I offer meal tickets for a job well done. If they starve, it's because they have parents who don't take their work seriously. What kind of boss would I be if I didn't offer consequences for actions?"

"You starve their children?" Bianca looks genuinely surprised, as though that horror goes beyond even what she thought him capable of. But I've seen the monster that lurks within River.

"They starve their children by not working. Come." He's clearly ready to dismiss the conversation, so I table it for now, though I intend on freeing every single one of these people by the time we leave here.

I'll free any who want that freedom…or I'll die trying.

We continue down the makeshift main street until we reach the edge of a massive pit in the ground. Going down at least a hundred feet if not more, there are stairs carved into the ground, and people are below, using tools to move through the dirt.

"You're looking for diamonds."

River turns to me, clearly impressed that I called it. "Good on you, SEAL. Yes, we *were* looking for diamonds. And we found them."

The people in the pit are sweaty and covered in dirt and grime. They're skin and bones, their faces gaunt, their expressions haunted. Armed guards patrol below in the pit and above, walking alongside the edges so not an inch of the place is unmonitored.

"So you kidnapped their children and put them to work in your mine?" Bianca whirls on him. "This is what you brought us here for? Because you've starved and worked these people to within an inch of their lives, and now you expect me to treat them?"

He doesn't even miss a beat. "Yes. I do. Now let me show you where you'll be working." Turning on his heel, he heads back toward the rows of converted shipping containers, stopping in front of the one closest to the pit. He opens the door and steps inside.

Bianca glances back at me, her emerald gaze furious, then follows him inside.

Yarrow shoves me so hard I nearly fall. Slowly, I turn to face him. "Have to come at me when my back is turned and my hands bound?"

"At the moment," Yarrow replies. "But we both know you're no match for me."

I grin, because truthfully? I hope I get to show him just how wrong he is. Then, because I know it'll make him even angrier, I don't say another word. I simply turn and follow Bianca into the medical building.

It's a crude room, with only four cots serving as hospital beds, and a wall of shelves containing medical supplies. There's a woman in the corner, her head bowed, hands trembling. Her dress is stained, the white apron she wears boasting a medical symbol.

"This is your nurse, Abana. She speaks English and will assist you in whatever way you need her to."

"It is a pleasure to meet you, Miss," Abana says, her accent thick.

"Call me Bianca," she replies, then turns to River. "Fine. But I can't help you while Silas is chained. So remove his handcuffs, give him a gun, and I'll get to work."

"A gun?" River laughs. "Do you think I'm stupid, girl? No. Your SEAL can protect you with his bare hands. I've seen him do it." He turns toward me. "Isn't that right, SEAL? Did he ever tell you about one of the times he got out?" He steps right up in my face. "I watched him—single-handedly—take out three of the highest-trained guards on your father's staff. Just leveled them like they were nothing."

"I was motivated," I growl.

"Oh, I imagine," River replies. "And I can also imagine just how motivated you are now, knowing what's on the line." He gestures to Bianca.

I don't give him the satisfaction of a response, just hold my wrists out so they can undo the handcuffs.

"This is a bad idea," Yarrow says. "I say we leave him chained."

"Don't be foolish," River replies. "He has a job to do, just as she does. Otherwise, why bring him?"

"My question exactly," Yarrow replies, keeping his gaze firm on me. "I think we should have thrown him out of the helicopter."

He removes the handcuffs, so I take a step closer to him, enjoying the clear fear his arrogance typically masks. "One day you're going to realize what a mistake it was to let me keep breathing."

Yarrow glares back at me, though he doesn't say anything.

"Easy, boys, we don't need to take this to violence. Do you need anything else?" River asks Bianca.

Yarrow steps back, retreating until he's at the door.

"Yes," Bianca replies, glaring back at her uncle. "A Bible."

CHAPTER 18
Bianca

"Okay, so where do we get our water?" I ask, turning to Abana.

"There's a well about a quarter mile from here. I can go retrieve your water, then bring it back and boil it over the fire," she says, gesturing toward a fireplace.

"A quarter mile?" *Unbelievable.* "It'll have to do. Are there any chronic illnesses we're dealing with?"

She shakes her head. "Though there is a pregnant woman. She is due to birth her child in a few weeks."

"He has a pregnant woman working in the mine pit?" I shouldn't be surprised after seeing those children starving to death on the streets. Yet here I am, once again shocked by the monsters in my bloodline.

"There is, Miss—"

"Bianca," I correct.

"Bianca," Abana repeats.

I can't free anyone just yet, so I'll control the things I

can. *Lord, please be with me. Please guide me so I can help these people and show them Your holy light. Amen.* I take a deep breath. "Okay. I want to see her first. Check her vitals and make sure the baby is okay. Where is she now?"

Abana looks at the small clock over the door. "Her shift will be over in thirty minutes."

"Shift? No. Go collect her now."

"Now?"

"Yes. I want her out of that pit now."

Abana tries to hide her smile. "Yes. I will do that. Excuse me," she says to Silas, then leaves the medical building.

Already exhausted, I rub both hands over my face.

"Are you all right?" Silas questions. He looks worn out too. He's taken up a post right beside the door. There are no windows, just muted light coming from the gas bulbs in the building. There's no air conditioning, no fan, just hot, humid air.

We might as well be inside a tin can.

"No. Not even a little." Closing my eyes, I take another deep breath. "But I will be, because I know God has this and we're not alone."

"Still with the faith, even as we're trapped in the depths of hell."

"I will have faith until the moment I draw my last breath, and then even still after."

"That powerful?"

"I feel Him, Silas." I press a hand to my chest. "Around me. In my heart. Months ago, something like this would have broken me, but now I know there's nothing to fear because no matter what, we're going to be fine."

"You feel so strongly you had them get a Bible for you."

I glance at the worn leather Bible on the table beside me. "Yes, I do. Sometimes you have to praise Him in the furnace," I say, repeating something Pastor Redding said to me a couple of weeks ago.

"Praise Him in the furnace?"

I smile. "You know the story of Daniel, right?"

"Man. The lions who didn't make a snack out of him. Yeah, I've heard it summarized."

Chuckling, I lift the Bible. "Shadrach, Meshach, and Abednego were three of Daniel's friends. They refused to worship a golden statue or the gods of a king. As punishment, the furnace was heated seven times hotter than normal, and the guards were ordered to bind Shadrach, Meshach, and Abednego, then throw them into the fire, fully clothed. It was so hot that it killed the guards who threw them in, but the three men were untouched by the flames. And when they looked into the furnace, they even saw a fourth in the fire with them."

Silas continues to stare at me. "God saved them."

"Yes," I reply. "He did. And it's yet more proof that no matter where you are, no matter what you face, His will is what will prevail. Not the will of man."

"Hmm," he grunts.

I open my mouth to respond, but the door swings open and Abana walks in with a *very* pregnant woman beside her. The woman is out of breath, her skin shimmering with sweat even as it's smeared with dirt.

"This is Laring," Abana says as she guides the woman over to one of the exam beds. The woman begins speaking in a language I can't understand, but thankfully, Abana is listening intently. "She is afraid. Doesn't understand why she's here when she should be working."

"She's here because she is far too pregnant to be working in the pit." I lift my stethoscope and slip it over my neck, then walk closer. "Can you tell her that she doesn't need to be afraid? I'll make sure she has food."

Abana repeats what I said, but the woman shakes her head and speaks again.

"She said that the boss will not tolerate her laziness."

"This is not laziness," I repeat. "You're posing a health risk to you and your baby, and I need to make sure that you're both healthy."

Abana repeats what I said, but the woman looks unconvinced.

"Have her lie back," I tell Abana.

Abana gives the order and the woman lies back.

"I'm going to give you privacy." Silas excuses himself, leaving just the three of us in the medical building.

I listen to the woman's heart, then use the stethoscope to listen to the baby's movements. When I hear the child alive within its mother's womb, I breathe a sigh of relief.

As soon as the exam is over, I step back and use the hand sanitizer in the corner to clean my hands. "The baby is healthy," I tell the women.

Abana translates, and the woman smiles, her eyes filling with tears.

"She says thank you," Abana replies.

"You're welcome. You both stay here. I'll be back in just a few minutes, okay?"

Abana nods, so I head for the door, shutting it behind me. Silas is nowhere to be found, and for a split second, my stomach turns into a pit of dread.

But then I hear yelling from the pit. Rushing forward, I find Silas standing in front of one of the guards, a worker behind him. The worker charges, and Silas holds him back. I sprint toward them.

"What's going on?" I demand.

"This is the husband of the woman you took to the medical building. He's worried about her."

"They both need to get back to work," the guard orders. "Now. Or I won't give any meal tickets to either of them."

I step up between Silas and the guard, going toe-to-toe with a man who stands a good four inches above me. "Listen here, I'm the doctor, and I'm telling you that Laring *will* be getting meal tickets, but she will *not* be working. Understand?"

The guard glares at me. "You're not in charge."

"I am of this. And as for her husband? It just so happens I'm in need of a second pair of strong hands, so he'll be coming with me."

"Again, you're not in charge." The guard moves closer, his gaze turning murderous.

I step forward and feel Silas right at my back. "Neither are you. And I'll be taking him with me."

"You have fun taking that up with River."

"I will." Turning toward the man, I offer him what I hope is a smile he'll understand. "Come," I say, reaching for his arm and gesturing toward the medical building. He eyes me warily, clearly confused, but soon he follows, and Silas falls into step beside me.

"You can't be picking fights with the guards, Bianca," Silas growls. "In case you forgot, I don't have a weapon."

"I'm not worried," I reply. "Because I'm doing what I'm supposed to."

We're nearly at the medical building when River and Yarrow step out of the house, both of them headed toward us. Yarrow speaks into a radio, and I imagine the guard at the top of the pit called it in.

Good.

"Go inside," I say, gesturing toward the door of the medical building. The last thing I want is this innocent man getting caught in the middle of this.

He looks from me to Silas, so I gesture toward the door again. This time, he understands, and pulls the door open, slipping inside. I step right in front of it, a challenge for Yarrow or River should they choose to deny what I'm about to request.

"Making waves on day one, huh?"

"It's what I do," I tell Silas. "Make them understand that I won't be pushed around, and they'll think twice before doing it."

He chuckles. "Smart woman."

"What is this I hear about you pulling two of my workers?" River questions.

"The woman is due to give birth any day now. She's not fit to be working in the pit. As for her husband, he needs to be with her, and I need an extra set of hands to get me water and fill my basins."

"Silas isn't cutting it?" Yarrow grins.

"Silas is my guard. He can't be leaving to get water."

"How about your nurse? We gave you one for this."

"I need Abana with me at all times for translation and an extra set of hands. I'll also be keeping the pregnant woman as a nurse before and after her baby is born. You'll ensure that she and her husband have enough meal tickets for themselves and their families."

River looks genuinely amused, but Yarrow looks about ready to blow a gasket.

"You make a lot of requests for a woman who's a prisoner here," Yarrow growls.

"I'm here to do a job, and if I can't do it effectively, why have me here at all?"

"You cannot be pulling my workers," River says. "I need them to meet my quota. Otherwise, this entire operation might as well go up in flames."

"Understood. But you can't expect me to run the only local hospital with only one extra set of hands."

He considers. "Fair enough. You may have the woman and her husband. But you take no others, understand?"

"They'll still get meal tickets?"

"Yes."

"They need an increase in whatever you're giving them."

River's amusement fades just slightly. "Excuse me?"

"She's eating for two, and by the looks of it, you're still only allowing her basic nutrition for her survival."

"Fine," River says. "But this is the last request you make of me. Do we understand each other?"

"We do."

"Boss, we need you on the south side of the fence, over," someone calls through the radio.

Yarrow lifts it. "On our way, over."

River continues staring at me a moment longer, then he and Yarrow turn and leave.

I let out a breath I hadn't realized I was holding.

"You good?" Silas questions.

"I am now. Come on, I need to get this woman cleaned up so she can be comfortable."

CHAPTER 19
Silas

"Okay, let's get you settled." Bianca guides Laring over to a medical bed on the far side of the converted storage container. The pregnant woman is glowing, her skin clear of sweat and grime, and she's been dressed in a clean dress the color of olives.

She smiles and thanks Bianca in her native language, as she covers her with a light blanket.

"You're welcome," Bianca replies, and Abana translates. She turns to the woman's husband, a man named Idra. "Can you please drain the tub? Then get some fresh water, and you can bathe as well."

Abana translates, and Idra grins widely and thanks her before rushing back toward the tub behind the partition that keeps it separate from everything else.

"You do good things for them," Abana says, eying Bianca curiously. "You are not like I thought you would be."

"How did you think I would be?" she asks.

"Like him," Abana replies. "Cold. Unfeeling. Evil."

Bianca flinches, but it's so slight I wonder if Abana even catches it. "I've dedicated my life to being nothing like him. I just wish I could help everyone."

"Perhaps you will," Abana replies after a moment.

The door opens, and Yarrow steps in. The mere sight of him sends my blood boiling. Especially when I see the way he looks at Bianca. To him, she's a prize to be won. A toy to be broken. But I'll die before I let him put his hands on her.

"What do you want?" she demands.

"We have a medical condition that needs to be seen to. In the pit."

"Bring them here," I tell him.

He looks at me. "Can't move him."

"Can't or won't?" she asks.

"Does it matter?"

Frustrated, Bianca grabs a bag she packed earlier and heads toward the door. "After you." She gestures for Yarrow to go out first.

I glance behind me at Abana's serious gaze. She hates Yarrow, that much is clear to see based on her expression. But she doesn't rush out the door. Are emergencies like this typical? What are we going to find?

Yarrow doesn't speak as he leads us toward the pit and down the crudely constructed wooden stairs. I keep glancing to my left and right, monitoring anyone who watches us. I don't believe this is a trap. If it is, it's a stupid

one and completely unnecessary given we're already pris-
oners, but I'm unwilling to rule anything out.

Not when Bianca's life depends on me being aware of
our surroundings.

A crowd's gathered at the bottom of the pit. Bianca
shoves through them fearlessly, while I do my best to
remain close enough that I can pull her out of harm's way.
We finally reach the center and find a man lying on his
back, his eyes frozen open.

A woman kneels beside him, tears in her eyes as she
grips his lifeless hand. She's devastated, broken as she
whispers into his ear.

You don't have to be a doctor to know the man is dead,
and as Bianca kneels, her delicate fingers checking for a
pulse, I already know she won't find one.

And based on the glare she gives Yarrow? She knew it
too. Bianca starts chest compressions, doing what she can
to bring the man back. She continues to work on him as
sweat beads on her brow, and yet he doesn't wake.

Finally, after what must have been nearly five minutes
of trying, Bianca stops. "How long has he been down?"

The woman begins speaking so fast that even if we
spoke her native tongue, we likely wouldn't have been
able to understand. She is screaming, crying, and furiously
pointing at Yarrow.

Yarrow rears back like he's going to strike her, so I step
in front of her, not speaking, though the challenge is
evident in my furious gaze. If he strikes her, I'll put him on
the ground.

"About fifteen minutes," he replies, glaring from me to Bianca.

"Fifteen minutes?" Bianca chokes out. "Was he still like this the entire time?"

Yarrow doesn't respond, and the woman kneeling continues screaming.

"He was moving until right before they went to get you," a man says, stepping from the crowd. His hair is gray, as is his beard, and both are coated in dirt. Kind, brown eyes stare back at us.

Yarrow glares at him, murder in his gaze.

"You mean to tell me that you left this man writhing on the ground for ten minutes before you came and got me?"

"Sometimes people get cramps," Yarrow replies. "Could have been a cramp."

"He's dead!" Bianca screams as she jumps to her feet. She starts for Yarrow, but I grip her good arm, keeping her from doing what we both want to do—slamming her fist into his jaw. "I might have been able to save him!"

Yarrow doesn't even flinch. In fact, he looks amused at her anger, and I wouldn't be surprised if he let this innocent man die just to spite Bianca for pulling Idra and Laring from their work. "Like you could have saved your father?" he asks.

Her hands tighten into fists at her sides, and she stiffens.

I release her.

"Toss the body," Yarrow orders.

Bianca steps in front of the deceased man. "You will not take him! He'll get a proper burial!"

"That's not how we do things here," Yarrow replies.

Bianca remains where she is, blocking the other guards from retrieving the body. I ready for a fight, preparing to protect Bianca at all costs.

"Get out of the way, Selena," he orders.

"No."

The woman who'd been kneeling beside the body remains where she is, too, even leaning in closer to Bianca.

Yarrow glares, clearly weighing his options.

If he forces Bianca away from the body, then she may cause trouble for him.

If he allows the direct violation of an order, that in itself could lead to problems.

Finally, he waves his hand in dismissal. "Fine. Do what you want with the body, but it better not be until after nightfall. You all have work to do. And don't forget about curfew. If you're caught out after hours, we'll dock your food." He turns and leaves, taking the two guards with him.

The man who'd translated steps forward. "We have a place," he says softly.

"Tell us where it is and we'll get him ready for burial," Bianca promises.

The man studies her, likely trying to discern whether or not he can trust her. The woman kneeling in the dirt sniffles and runs her hand over the side of the dead man's face. My heart aches for her, a tightness spreading through my chest and into my gut.

To love means to eventually lose.

I know that better than most.

My gaze falls on Bianca.

But is that a reason to not love at all?

<hr>

BIANCA STANDS BESIDE ME, SILENT AS THE BODY IS LOWERED into the ground by two men. Cloaked in linen, the body was washed and prepared for burial by Bianca and Abana, both women working hard to ensure he regained the dignity stolen from him by River and Yarrow.

A man speaks in their foreign language, but Abana translates for us in a low whisper.

"Shaene was a good man. Honest. Kind. A friend to all. May he rest in peace now, knowing that his life will forever be remembered," she whispers. "His wife will rest peacefully knowing she will one day see him, as will his children."

As she speaks, my gaze drifts to the woman who'd knelt beside him. She stands with her children, a boy and a girl, both no older than thirteen. The girl and her mother are in tears, while the boy is trying his hardest to remain strong.

That bottled-up strength is something I understand quite well.

Bianca sniffles, and I look over as she wipes a tear from her cheeks.

Without giving it the thought I probably should, I reach out and take her hand with mine, interweaving our fingers. The touch does more for me than I can even put into words, the warmth of the contact shooting straight up through my arm, and I know—without a doubt—that I can do anything as long as she's with me.

"May I?" Bianca asks as soon as the man is done speaking.

Abana translates and the man nods, gesturing for her to speak. She pulls her hand from mine and opens her Bible. "I'm new here, but I see the pain you are all suffering. I see the agony that weighs you down, and I'm praying harder than I've ever prayed for you to all regain the freedom that was stolen from you." She pauses so Abana can continue translating. "I wish to read you part of a Psalm that brings me comfort when I'm weighed down by pain."

Abana finishes, and a woman calls something out. Abana turns to us. "She asks what is a Psalm."

Bianca's eyes widen, and I can see that she's struggling to find the words to explain. I start to respond with what little I know, but she begins speaking before I can. "We are all created by a loving God. And while we face many trials in this life, His Son, Jesus Christ, came and died for our sins so that we may one day join Him in His kingdom." She holds up her Bible. "This is the Holy Bible. It is God's Word. His law and His promises. The Psalms were mainly written by a man named David. He was a shepherd, but God made him a king."

The group around us is focused on her intently. They hang on every single word she speaks. "This is from Psalm 34." She clears her throat. "'The eyes of the Lord are on the righteous, and his ears are attentive to their cry; but the face of the Lord is against those who do evil, to blot out their name from the earth. The righteous cry out, and the Lord hears them; he delivers them from all their troubles. The Lord is close to the brokenhearted and saves those who are crushed in spirit. The righteous person may have many troubles, but the Lord delivers him from them all; protects all his bones, not one of them will be broken. Evil will slay the wicked; the foes of the righteous will be condemned. The Lord will rescue his servants; no one who takes refuge in him will be condemned.'"

There is not a single word uttered amongst those listening, and even as difficult a concept as faith has been for me, I can *see* a bit of hers taking root in each of the people standing before me.

Their expressions are a mixture of fear and hope.

Of love and understanding. Like they've been waiting for these words their entire lives.

A woman speaks, and Abana turns to Bianca. "She asks if you truly believe there is such a God who will deliver us from this pain."

"Yes," Bianca replies without hesitation. "I do."

Abana continues staring at her. "You believe, yet you are prisoner here, too."

"Not for long," Bianca replies, then reaches out to gently touch Abana's arm. "And when I leave, you'll all be free too."

CHAPTER 20

Bianca

A chill clings to the air around us, and I tug the small blanket up closer around my neck, then roll to my side. I'd moved my cot closest to the bars separating Silas and I, wanting to be closer to him and not caring if it makes me look weak.

I'm terrified.

Because I know that if we don't find a way to escape, there's no chance River is letting us go home. He'll kill us, bury our bodies here, and never think about it again.

I study Silas's profile in the dim light, but I can't make out much. I do see that his eyes are closed, his breathing soft. Is he awake? Or did he finally catch the same sleep I'm desperately chasing?

It's far too dark to read my Bible, thanks to the single dim light over the door leading up to the main house, but I still clutch the book to my chest, running my fingers over the pages for comfort. We buried a man today.

Rescued two from the pit—for now.

And I promised them all I would help them get free.

How I'm supposed to do that, I'm not sure. But I know that one day, I'll see their freedom. Somehow. I *feel* it.

"You awake?"

"Yeah," I reply.

Silas stands and grips his cot, then drags it across the floor until he's right beside the bars—mere inches from me. Without another word, he lies down on his back and puts his right arm behind his head.

"You got to those people today."

I smile into the darkness. "You think?"

"I do. What you said meant a lot to them. Especially after everything they've been through. You gave them hope."

"God's Word gave them hope," I reply. "I merely read the words."

"You did more than that," Silas replies. "You also promised them freedom."

"I did." I sigh. "Not sure how I'll manage that one."

"I'll help you."

I look over at him again. "You will?"

He turns to look at me. "Can't let you have all the fun, can I?" The ghost of a smile graces his handsome face and my heart skips as my stomach warms.

"I guess not."

Silas smiles. "Tell me about your mother."

"What? Why?"

"When we were in the jungle, I talked about my family.

My parents, sister—but you never said anything about yours. Now, I get why you never mentioned your father or uncle, but what about your mother? Do you have any siblings?"

As it always does, the mere thought of my mother brings a heavy wave of grief over me. But this time, now that I've found peace through God, the weight is a bit less, and I catch myself smiling softly.

"She made the best pancakes in the world. We had a woman who cooked for us, but every Saturday morning, my mother would make pancakes, bacon, and eggs."

"What I wouldn't give for a pancake right now," Silas jokes.

"I know." I laugh. "My stomach is growling just talking about it. I'd wake up to the scent of breakfast cooking, and come rushing down the stairs. No matter how old I got, it was the best part of my week. Saturday mornings with my mom. That and the crunchy peanut butter I'd smear all over my pancakes."

"Crunchy peanut butter?" he asks, making a disgusted face that has me laughing.

"Don't knock it till you try it, Williamson. When we get out of here, I'm taking you to the diner and you're going to try it."

He grins. "It's a date."

My heart leaps in my chest. Have things truly shifted this drastically between us? Or is the change just because we once again find ourselves only able to rely on each other?

"Do you look like her?" he asks suddenly.

"I think so?" I say. "To be honest, I'm not entirely sure. She was always so beautiful and feminine. There was a softness about her, even though I knew she could be tough as nails when she needed to be."

"It sounds like you're just like her."

Butterflies fill my stomach at his compliment, and I no longer feel like a girl in the midst of a nightmare, but rather a foolish teen with her first crush.

Silas Williamson does that to me.

"She was a good person. I struggled though, for a long time after her death. Trying to understand why she would marry a man like Lucian."

"People make mistakes."

"That they do," I reply. "But that seemed like such a large one."

"Maybe she didn't know who he was."

"I think she knew parts of it," I admit. "I think on some level, she believed she could fix him. When I was younger, she'd push for us to go on these vacations. No guards, no phones, no communication with anyone outside of our family. I think she was trying to get him to see what life could be like if he left everything else behind."

"There's another thing you two have in common."

"What's that?" I ask, turning to look at him again, only this time I find him watching me. The intensity of his gaze, even in the dim light of this prison, knocks the breath from my lungs.

"You both think you can fix everyone. Her with him, you with me."

"I'm not trying to fix you, Silas."

"No?"

"You're not broken. You think you are, and perhaps pieces of you are chipped, but you're still the best man I know. Strong, courageous, kind…willing to sacrifice everything for the innocent."

He looks away from me. "You don't know the anger I carry, Bianca. The weight of it all."

"Then tell me about it." This is the most open he's ever been with me, and I'm almost afraid to respond. Whether it's fear that we won't survive this or loneliness driving him to open up, I don't care. The why doesn't matter. Just that he is.

"I'm angry about what happened to my team. They were good men. Men who had families and futures. They should have grown to be old men watching their grandchildren play in the yard." He falls silent a moment, but since I sense he's not done, I don't say anything. "And my sister, what sense is it that she died? She had a little girl to take care of, she'd just gotten her dream job, bought her first house, and then she was gone, just like that." He snaps his fingers.

"I wish I had an answer for you. For all of it."

"You've suffered. Lost your mother. How can you have such faith when faced with so much pain?"

I consider his question because I know that my answer carries a weight even I can't fully comprehend. "Because I know that there will come a time when pain will be no more. When God will wipe the tears from our eyes and grant us more peace and comfort than we can even imagine. I know that even though we suffer here, He won't leave us in it. Even if we can't see the end of the tunnel, it's there."

"How can you cling to your faith like that? How do you know?"

I consider his question, trying to come up with an answer that will make sense to him. "Truthfully, it's a feeling. I don't know how else to put it into words. I just *feel* the promise. The peace in knowing God's Word to be fact."

"I still only see words on paper."

"I was like that, too, you know," I tell him. "I actually started out reading a Bible on my tablet because I couldn't understand how Lance had such faith. How he brought Eliza into it and helped Michael, Elijah, and Jaxson with theirs. It didn't make sense to me."

"I didn't know that."

"I didn't tell anyone I was reading it because I was embarrassed that I didn't feel the same connection everyone else did. But after I learned that River was after me, that my old life was haunting me all over again, I found myself standing outside the church because I *felt* like it's where I was supposed to go. A voice in my head telling me that it's okay. That even if I'm not a Sunday morning girl, I was still welcome."

"Did you go in?"

"Not alone. Pastor Redding was on his way out. He

asked me to come inside, and even though I wanted to walk away, I couldn't ignore the feeling in my chest, a weight that told me to take another step forward, so I did."

"So Pastor Redding taught you to believe."

"Pastor Redding offered me a place to rest. A place to lay the pain, stress, and heaviness of life. Somewhere I didn't have to be strong. I could just be the daughter of a King. The daughter of a God who, even as society screams otherwise, chose me even before He knit me together in my mother's womb." I think back to Psalm 139. About the peace I found when I read it.

"And it was that easy."

I snort. "There's nothing easy about it," I tell him. "It feels like the second I started really believing and actively seeking my relationship with Him, the world came crumbling down around me even more so than it already was."

"How do you explain that then?" Silas asks as he gets to his feet and begins to pace. "Why would God punish you for believing in Him?"

"He's not punishing me," I reply. "It's not Him causing my pain. And while it took me a bit to see that, I understand it now. In those moments, when everything feels like it's smothering me and the weight of the world is crushing, I turn to God. I ask Him for strength, for hope."

"Does He deliver?"

"Yes."

"We're still here."

"But look at what we can accomplish." I get to my feet as well and move toward the bars where Silas stands. "The people we can help. The peace we can bring them." Hope spreads through me like wildfire, igniting me with purpose. I reach forward and touch his forearm through the bars. "Silas, we can save these people. We can bring them God. Freedom. Hope. Peace. Security."

Silas stares back at me, his expression unreadable. He could think I'm insane, and while that would suck, I'm fully prepared for it because I found a reason in my pain. A chance to fight for good in the middle of this nightmare.

Silas steps closer to the bars and stares down at me, his eyes full of emotion. He reaches up and brushes strong fingers over my cheek. I shiver at the touch, at the tenderness. "I don't know how I feel about God," he admits softly. "But I'm glad you've found peace, Bianca. I truly am."

"Open your heart, Silas, and you can find peace, too."

He smiles. "I'm learning that anything is possible." He drops his hand and returns to his cot.

I do the same, lying back and staring up at the ceiling.

Silas reaches through the bars and takes my hand, linking his fingers with mine as we lie side-by-side, separated by iron and four inches of space.

"No matter what, I promise you that I'll help you free these people," he says. "Even if it means neither of us leave this place, I can die knowing I tried to make a difference. I think Eloise could be proud of that."

I close my eyes and take a deep breath, clinging to his hand like a tether.

"Eloise will always be proud of you, Silas, but we'll make it home so you can share the story yourself."

Lord, please soften Silas's heart. Please reach him and help him see the truth that his peace can only be found with You. Lord, please use me to bring these people to freedom. Please use me to help them find You and Your truth. God, please let our time here mean something. I ask this in Jesus' name. Amen.

A tear rolls down my cheek, but I don't wipe it away. I let it fall, slipping down my face and onto the cot beneath me as I drift off to sleep.

CHAPTER 21
Silas

My entire body is shaking by the time I come out of the nightmare. I can't make it stop, every inch of me shivering uncontrollably. My teeth chatter, and I try desperately to keep quiet so I don't wake Bianca who is sleeping a few feet away from me.

But I can't stop.

I can still feel the blade slipping into my skin, the searing pain of it as River reopens the wound again and again. My breathing is ragged, and I grip the soft grass beneath me, hoping to ground the panic.

"Hey, easy." Then Bianca is there, her hands going to either side of my head as she cradles me, her fingers delicately stroking my skin. "Breathe, Silas, it's okay. You're safe."

Safe? Is she crazy? We're not safe. We're out here in the open, trapped in the backyard of a killer. How is that safe?

"Breathe," she says again, her emerald gaze locking on mine. Even with only the light of the moon overhead to grant me *visibility, I lock onto her beautiful face. To the calmness in her expression.*

And I press the heel of my palm to my chest, just above my heart.

I breathe. Deep breath in, deep breath out.

"There you go, it's going to be okay," she coos. "Just keep focused on me, Silas. Always stay focused on me."

"Okay, I think everything is where I want it now." Hands on her hips, Bianca studies the medical cabinet she just logged and organized. Abana is beside her, making notes on a clipboard, which she then offers to Bianca. "It's not everything I would typically want, but it'll do."

Idra is out gathering water, while Laring sits in a chair in the corner, humming softly and running her hand over her belly. I can't help but feel a bit of joy when I look over and see how relaxed she is.

Bianca did that. Bianca pulled her and her husband out of that pit, fought for them to stay here, and pushed back so a woman could bury her husband rather than allowing Yarrow to discard the body the same way they did my teammates all those years ago.

She's an incredible woman.

Bianca turns and catches me watching her. Her cheeks flush. "What?"

"Nothing. Just admiring your work," I say, gesturing to the cabinet.

"Oh. Well, I figured if I'm going to do a job, I might as well do it right. Wait, how much gauze do we have?" she asks, then checks the clipboard.

"I'm going to step outside a moment."

"Okay," Bianca replies.

Since there's only one door in and out of this place, I don't worry as I step out of the door and onto the dirt street, though I remain right beside the door as I study the area. As we were escorted here this morning, I'd looked for weak spots in their defenses.

So far, unfortunately, I've found none. River runs a tight ship, just as Lucian did all those years ago. The fence around the camp is topped with razor wire, the dirt beneath it hard enough it would take tools and a lot of manpower or time to dig our way out.

Guards patrol consistently, and when I was out here two hours ago, I noticed they were rotating locations. Which it looks like they're doing now. No long assignments here, no chance for the guards to get complacent.

I turn my attention to the pit.

Guards patrol above, shouting orders occasionally or just yelling expletives at the people working down inside. It infuriates me, but I know there's nothing I can do about it...yet.

"Hey!"

I shift my attention to a group of kids as they rush over toward me. Two boys, who look to be around ten, three younger ones who are likely six or seven, and a little girl who appears to be around Eloise's age.

My chest aches thinking of her. I miss her. So, so much.

"Hey," I reply.

A boy in front of the group, wearing tattered pants and a tan linen shirt, looks up at me curiously. "You are American, yes?" he asks.

"I am. You speak good English."

He beams at me. "My mother was teaching me before —" He gestures to this, and I see anger blossom on his young face.

"How did this happen?" I question.

"They just showed up one day," the boy answers. "And they promised that my parents would be rich. That we could buy whatever we wanted. So we let them put up their buildings." He points to the house at the end of the street. "That was mine," he says, pressing his hand to his chest. "It's the only home they left standing."

Fury sings through my veins. "They destroyed your homes?"

He nods. "Tore them down to put up these." He gestures to the metal buildings lining the street. "I hear you are a SEAL. Is that true?"

"I was."

"Are you here to save us?"

The weight of that question settles on my shoulders, so I squat down, putting myself just below eye level of the boy. "I'm going to do my best."

The boy nods, then looks back as the little girl curls against his side. "This is my sister, Zela."

"Hi, Zela. You know, I have a niece about your age," I tell her.

She smiles.

"She doesn't speak any English," the boy says, then translates. The little girl's smile widens and she asks a question. "She wants to know what her name is."

"Eloise," I reply. Just speaking her name makes that pain return. What is she doing right now? Is she wondering where I am? Why I left? "I miss her very much."

The little boy plants his hand on my shoulder. "You will see her again," he says. "I believe that."

I can't help but smile. "Thank you for that." He nods, and I stand. "What is your name?" I question, realizing he introduced his sister, but not himself.

"Neo," he replies.

I offer my hand. "It's good to meet you, Neo."

"You, too, SEAL."

"Silas," I reply.

"Silas," the boy repeats, then tilts his head to the side and studies me. "I think I want to still call you SEAL."

I laugh. "Go for it, kid."

Another boy in the back leans forward and whispers something to Neo. He listens intently, then nods and returns his attention to me. "My friend has a question."

"Okay. Go for it."

"We were at the funeral last night, and he wants to know what that woman was talking about."

My stomach twists because I have a feeling I know what he's getting at. "What do you mean?"

"She spoke of Lord and joining Him in His kingdom. What does that mean?"

I start to turn toward the building to grab Bianca. After all, she's much more qualified to answer this than I am, but seeing the hope on their faces, the interest, I can't bring myself to step away. Who am I to squash the seed of faith Bianca helped plant?

So even though I have no idea if what I will say is accurate, I kneel. "She was talking about God," I tell him. "The Bible tells us that God sent His Son to die on the cross so that we might find eternal life with Him."

"He sent His Son to die? Why?"

"Because people are wicked," I tell him, gesturing to the street around us. "They do wicked things like lie, cheat, steal—"

"Kill?" Neo asks.

I swallow hard. "That too. But if we ask for forgiveness, believing that our only way into heaven is through the death and sacrifice of Jesus Christ, and we work really hard to try and follow His way and get to know Him, then we can join Him in His kingdom someday."

Neo beams. "A kingdom?"

I nod. "Bianca knows more about it than I do, but that sounds pretty nice, doesn't it?"

"It does!" he exclaims, then turns to translate to the others.

The children's faces completely light up, their expressions turning brilliant. They all begin talking at once and Neo laughs, then turns back to me.

"They are quite excited about it."

"I can see that."

"Do you know if she will read us more? We want to know more about Jesus," he says. "We want to hear more."

"I'm sure she will," I reply, standing once more. Warmth spreads through my chest, happiness at the smiles I put on their faces by not turning away. So much hope, so much joy… Why can't I find that for myself in the word of God? Why can't I put aside my pain to push forward?

Commotion near the pit draws my attention, and the kids turn and sprint down the street, with Neo lifting his little sister and carrying her off and out of view.

I shift my gaze toward the pit, watching as a man climbs out.

The guard raises his weapon toward the man, and I sprint forward, dread coiling in my stomach.

"Get back in the pit!" the guard orders. "I will shoot!"

I pump my arms faster, running as quickly as I can. "Stop!" I yell. "He doesn't understand you!"

Though I can't imagine that's entirely true—having a gun pointed at you is a universal language most understand. The ferocity in the man's eyes, the fury reflected in them is also a universal language.

He doesn't care if he lives or dies.

But I do.

All of these people need to live so they can enjoy peace again. I slam into the man, taking him to the ground. Pain shoots through my gut, but I ignore it as the man squirms, trying to break free. "Stop!" I yell. "You're going to get yourself killed!" When he doesn't stop moving or yelling, I call out, "Translator!"

The same man who'd translated in the pit yesterday rushes forward.

My vision wavers. Did I hit my head?

Suddenly, the world begins to spin, and I fall back, breathing ragged. I suck in a breath, but the air doesn't come. The man's face swims into view above me. He's talking fast, too fast for me to understand.

I look down at my gut and see that the man I tackled was not unarmed. Something I should have noticed well before taking him to the ground.

A rusty knife sticks out of my chest. The guard reaches down and rips it free, glaring at the man who'd stabbed me. A man who is staring down at me with horror in his gaze.

The translator presses his hands to my chest and yells an order, but I can't tell if anyone moves. All I can feel is the blood pouring out of my chest, and the world around me growing dark. Is this how I die?

Cool fingers grip me, pulling me under, and I'm surrounded by darkness.

Screaming.

Tormented voices.

Shadows fill my vision. They cling to me like ink, but I'm too weak to move, so I just lay there as they cover me.

Please, no. I try to speak, but nothing comes out. *Please don't let me leave Bianca. She needs me. The people there need me.*

But the shadows don't respond, even when I open my mouth to try and scream.

Then—"*You belong to Me.*" The Powerful proclamation echoes through my mind at the same time a bright light pierces the dark, and the shadows retreat, racing away from me as the light fully encompasses everything around me. Then there's nothing—just light.

And an overwhelming sense of peace.

CHAPTER 22
Bianca

"Okay, this is good, right?" I say as I stand back from the cabinet after moving a few things. I'm not entirely sure why I felt the need to reorganize everything, but I need to know where everything is.

If there's an emergency, the seconds spent searching for something could mean life or death.

"It's good," Abana replies. "You do good work."

I snort. "All I did was organize."

"Today, you organized. But yesterday you brought Laring and Idra comfort. Who knows what you will do tomorrow?"

"Who knows," I reply with a half-smile.

The door flies open and I whirl, expecting to see Silas telling me that Lance and the others are here. That the cavalry has arrived and we're going home. Instead, it's a ten-year-old boy, his eyes wild and afraid.

"Come!" he yells. "The SEAL needs you!"

"The SEAL? Silas!" I grab the closest medical bag—one of the things I just repacked and organized—and sprint out the door. My boots hit the dirt in heavy strides as I race toward the pit. But I don't have to go far.

Two men, one who translated for me yesterday and another I don't recognize, are carrying a limp Silas, while Idra applies pressure to a wound in his chest. Dread turns my stomach to a pit of rocks.

Please, God, no. Not him. Please don't take him.

"Get him inside," I order.

They listen, taking him over toward the cot closest to the door. They set him down, and I grip the front of his blood-soaked T-shirt and tear, ripping the fabric open. Blood is pouring from a wound in his chest.

"I need to know what happened. Alcohol," I order Abana as I press fresh gauze onto the injury in Silas's chest, holding pressure there until she returns.

I try not to look at his face, forcing myself to keep my attention only on his injury. Because I know that if I look up at him, I'll lose it. Something he can't afford.

She retrieves the bottle, and I pour it onto another stack of gauze, then work cleaning the area around the wound. "Keep pressure," I tell her.

She replaces my hands and I continue cleaning the area so I can make sure there's just the one injury. My training kicks in, and I work down my list. Life-threatening injuries first. So far, thank God, it looks like it's just the one.

"You can answer at any time!" I call out.

"He tried to intervene in a fight with a guard and was stabbed," the translator finally says.

"With what?"

"A knife. The guard ripped it out and confiscated it."

"He pulled the knife out?" I snap, dipping my hands into the clean water basin, drying them with more gauze, and pulling gloves on.

The man nods.

Anger burns hot through me. Anyone with any common sense knows you don't remove something when it's punctured the body. Not until a doctor has a chance to evaluate and remove it themselves. Which means either the guard is an idiot, or he didn't care.

Either reason infuriates me.

"Which guard stabbed him?" No one answers, so I look up at them. "Which guard?" I snap.

The translator looks at the man standing beside him. His eyes are wide, red, and full of tears. "Not a guard," the translator says.

Silas wheezes, a horrifying sound that alerts me to internal injuries. "The blade must have pierced his lung," I tell Abana. With shaking hands, I dig into my bag, searching for the stethoscope. After placing it in my ears, I press the diaphragm against Silas's chest. His breathing is faint and strained, his pulse racing so fast I'm worried his heart' going to burst. "It's collapsed, and I need to get the air out. Get me some iodine and a chest tube from the cabinet."

She leaves my side, only to return a few moments

later. I move around Silas's side, cleaning the spot with iodine before making a small incision. I take the tube and shove it into the pleural space around his lung, praying that it's enough to alleviate the pressure in his chest. Without any kind of imaging equipment, all I have is a shot in the dark.

I suppose it's a good thing I spent most of my career as a medic making exactly these kinds of calls in the field. An easy thing to do when it's nameless soldiers on a battlefield. But this is Silas.

Please, Lord. Please guide me. Don't take him away.

Air rushes out through the tube mere seconds before the liquid begins to drain, and he sucks in a breath.

"Hold him down!" I yell as he tries to jolt up off the table.

Idra, the translator, and the man who stabbed him rush over, each of them gripping Silas and pinning him to the table as the rest of the air in his thoracic cavity releases.

"Just breathe, Silas," I tell him. "Please breathe."

He draws in a breath, though it's strained.

Putting my stethoscope back in my ears, I place the diaphragm onto Silas's chest again, listening to his breath sounds. They're better. Still not great, but better. But it's enough that I can work on stitching his skin back together.

I take a moment to steady myself, taking a deep breath, then head over to my cabinet. As far as pain meds go, there's practically nothing. The strongest we have is ibuprofen, and since that won't do anything right now, I walk over to Silas.

He's staring up at me, green eyes wide. "I don't have anything to numb the area around the wound."

"Just do it," he wheezes, closing his eyes.

I look up to the men. "I need to make sure there's nothing foreign in the wound, then stitch it back together. It's going to hurt—badly—and I need you to hold him still."

Abana translates before the other man can, and Idra and the man who stabbed Silas both nod. Abana turns to me. "Tell me what you need."

TWO HOURS LATER, THE WOUND IS SUTURED, A BAG HAS BEEN placed near the chest tube still in his side, and I've given a round of IV antibiotics to prevent any infection. Silas is asleep, and Abana, Idra, and Laring have all retreated to their bunkhouses, along with the translator and the man who'd stabbed Silas.

Just thinking about him angers me, even though the translator insists it wasn't done on purpose.

Night has fallen just outside, and I'm sitting at the table reading my Bible. We should be going back to the house so they can place us in our cells, but I can't bring myself to wake Silas when he finally managed to sleep.

The door opens, and River walks in. His gaze lands on Silas before he turns to me and nods. "Glad to see he's still breathing."

I don't dignify him with a response.

"I heard what happened at the pit today. Next time, Silas needs to remain out of the arguments. They happen often, sometimes resulting in death or punishment. Other times, they fizzle out. Either way, it's not his place."

"Tell your guards that the next time one of them removes a weapon embedded in an injury, they'll answer for it," I reply, ignoring his warning.

"Fair enough." He crosses his arms. "You two didn't gather your meal tickets. Did you forget how it was explained to you?"

"Does it look like he can be moved?" I demand.

River's gaze hardens. "I allowed you to take the pregnant woman and her husband off of my crew. Then Yarrow allowed you to bury that man rather than disposing of his body in a way that saved time. But do not mistake those kindnesses for weakness."

"There isn't a kind bone in your body," I growl. "Just like there wasn't in my father's."

"Your father was the greatest man I knew."

"Why? Because he pulled you out of a drug house and threw you into a life of crime? Yeah, real winner, that one."

River's gaze turns murderous, angrier than I've ever seen him. He crosses over toward where Silas is sleeping. I get up, setting my Bible aside and gripping the scalpel I left beside me. "It would be so easy to kill him now," River says. "Make you watch as the last of his life left his body."

"Don't you dare touch him."

Silas's eyes open, but he remains where he is, unmoving as River hovers over him.

"Then you'd better remember who is in charge, Bianca, because if you question me again, I'll kill him and let you fend for yourself amongst these animals."

We both know Silas is here as leverage for me. I'm not foolish enough to truly believe River thought these people were violent enough that I would need a security guard. Which means he'll kill Silas if given the motive. I can't give that to him. So I swallow my anger and pride.

"I'm sorry," I say, each word paining me to speak it.

"Good girl. Now that he's awake, I suggest you two get back to the house so you can be placed securely in your cells until morning. It's late, and I'm getting cranky."

"I have to check out the injury, and then we'll be back."

"Fantastic." River smiles. "I'll be stationing a guard outside to escort you back. Feel free to give him an earful about the weapon, as he's the one who removed it from our favorite SEAL here." River turns to leave. "And another thing. Remember my warning, Bianca, because you won't get another one."

As soon as he's out, Silas sits up on the cot, hissing through clenched teeth as he does. I cross over toward him.

"Are you all right?" he asks, still a bit out of breath. Which he will be for about a week or two, depending on how bad the lung collapse was. As it stands, the tube will have to remain in place for a few days still.

"Fine. How do you feel?" I put the ear pieces for my stethoscope into my ears, then press the diaphragm against his chest so I can hear his heart.

"Bianca." Silas's hand caresses my cheek, and my blood warms. I look up at him, and everything I'd been trying so hard to bury for the day comes rushing back. Tears fill my eyes, and I wrap both arms around his waist, leaning my head against his chest.

"For a second, I thought you were dead."

"I think I might have been for a second there," he replies, voice raspy.

"What do you mean?" I pull away, staring up at him. He continues caressing my cheek.

"Let's just say I had my eyes opened a bit," he replies. "And I'm trying to open them the rest of the way."

CHAPTER 23

Silas

THREE WEEKS LATER

"That should do it." Bianca runs her arm over her forehead, wiping away the sweat from her brow as she studies the stitches she just finished on a child who tripped and fell, slicing open his forearm.

Abana translates what Bianca said, and the little boy looks down at his arm, then beams up at Bianca, before telling her "thank you". She smiles.

"You are so welcome. Maybe next time don't try and jump from one building to another. In fact, stay off the roof altogether." She pats him on the back and he beams up at her.

Abana translates and the little boy laughs and nods. He hugs Bianca, then heads for the door, likely to try the very thing she told him not to do.

In the last three weeks, I've managed to pick up some of the more common phrases, especially thanks to Neo, who's taken it upon himself to help me learn, though I'm not nearly as fast a learner as Bianca. The woman has an ear for languages. Just one of her many impressive qualities.

She rolls her shoulders and starts cleaning off the table, sanitizing it and sticking her tools in a bucket to get cleaned before reuse. River's budget unfortunately doesn't call for brand-new sterilized tools when it comes to the people here who Bianca helps. He and Yarrow, however, have their own separate stash.

"Are you feeling all right?" Abana asks.

"Yeah, just tired. I didn't get much sleep last night." Bianca takes a seat at the small two-seater table, and Idra places a mug of water in front of her. She smiles up at him. "Thank you."

He nods, then lifts the water bucket and heads out the door to swap it out, just as he does after each patient Bianca sees. Aside from my injury, Bianca has helped a handful of kids, three men injured in the pit, and two women who suffered heat stroke over the past three weeks.

No one else has died—thankfully.

In fact, they're all in even better spirits than before we arrived, and we haven't even figured out how to get them free yet. Bianca reading to them from the Bible each night during dinner, with Abana translating, has changed the way they see things.

She's changed the way I see things, too. Ever since I nearly died and heard that voice, I've been actively seeking the same connection with God, but so far I'm still struggling. In the quiet, when Bianca is sleeping, I try talking to Him. But I get nothing in return.

It's like He's uninterested in me. Though I know that's not true. He saved me, something I don't doubt in the least, and I have to believe it was for a reason.

Things with Bianca are improving, at least. I no longer hang on to that anger I carried for her. Truth is, I realized I've actually been angry at myself for not being there when Sierra died. I should have been there, home with her. But because I was so broken up over Bianca and what I'd gone through, I'd locked myself in that cabin. Then blamed Bianca for the fact that Sierra died before I could get home to her.

Now, when I look at Bianca, I no longer feel that anger I carried for all those years. Nor do I feel pain. All I feel is—

Bianca runs her arm back over her forehead, then closes her eyes.

I narrow my gaze, noting the paleness of her complexion. She's been off today, a bit more fatigued than normal. But given we're going on nearly a month here, I assumed it was just the stress of everything. What if I'm wrong though? "Bianca, I think you need to rest."

"I'm sitting now," she insists.

"Maybe you need to go back to the cell and lie on the cot." It may be a prison cell, but it's a lot cooler down there than it is up here.

"Nah, I'll be fine."

"Bian—"

"Silas, I promise. I need to stay here until after dinner time. Then I'll get a good night's sleep and bounce back to a hundred and ten percent tomorrow." But even as she says it, I can see she doesn't entirely believe those words. Her eyes are glossy and unfocused, her skin paling even further as each second passes.

Abana reaches forward and presses her wrist to Bianca's forehead. "You are feverish," she says.

"Feverish?" I rush forward and feel her forehead. She's hot to the touch, hotter than I remember Eloise being the first time she got the flu. And her temperature had spiked at 103. "Do you have a thermometer?" I ask Abana.

She nods and plucks one from the first aid kit.

"I don't need that," Bianca insists.

"Stop protesting," Abana orders.

Bianca opens her mouth and Abana slips the thermometer into her mouth. I remain where I am, watching as the red color grows higher and higher on the old school mercury thermometer.

"104.1," Abana says as she pulls the thermometer out of Bianca's mouth.

Bianca simply waves her away. "It's hot in here. I bet if you checked Silas he'd read the same."

"You're ill. We need to get you out of here," Abana says.

"No. I have people to help," she replies, her expression turning stubborn.

"You can't help them if you're dead," I insist.

"We can manage," Abana assures her. "You've been training Laring, and we have Idra as well."

"No. This is my—" Bianca no sooner stands than she's swaying on her feet, her eyes rolling back in her head. I lunge forward, catching her as she collapses.

"Bianca!" I yell, running my hands over her face. She doesn't move.

Doesn't stir.

And I feel the fear of what may come next piercing my bones. "Wake up! Bianca!"

"Here, try this." Abana parts Bianca's lips and pours some water inside.

It simply pools and pours down the side of her face.

"What's happening?"

Abana feels her forehead again. "She's too hot. We need to cool her down. Her fever is spiking."

"How?" The main house doesn't have running water, so a cool bath is out of the question. Everything comes from the well, and it's always warm.

She looks to Laring as the woman says something I can't understand.

Abana nods. "We know a place. A spring that has cool water. But the guards will never allow us to leave."

The door opens, and Idra walks in, humming a happy song that dies the moment he sees us kneeling on the floor. He rushes over and sets the bucket of water down, then kneels next to me, his hand taking Bianca's.

"Where?"

"It's not in this camp," she says.

"I don't care. Can you take us there?"

"If you get us permission to leave, I will take you there."

"Done." I cradle Bianca against me and stand, then head out the still-open door, Abana, Idra, and Laring behind me.

I rush outside, moving as fast as I can as I cradle her against my chest. "Hang on, Bianca, you better not die on me."

She groans in response, her head lolling to the side. Sweat beads on her face, and I imagine her temperature climbing. The guard outside of the main house steps in front of the door, blocking my way as soon as I step up onto the porch.

"I need to speak with River. It's urgent."

He looks from Bianca to me. "No."

I step closer. "Do you see her? She's sick, and I need to speak with River."

"No. I'm not allowed to let anyone into this house."

I turn toward Idra. "Take her."

Even though we don't speak the same language, he clearly understands and takes Bianca into his arms. I turn back toward the guard, stepping even closer now as I clench my hands into fists at my sides. "I am getting through that door. It's up to you if you want to remain standing."

"Is that a threat?" he asks.

"It's a promise. Move."

He opens his mouth to respond, but the door opens behind him.

"What's this, then?" River questions.

The guard moves quickly. "He was trying to get inside."

Bianca's uncle looks past me at her, his gaze widening just a bit before he shifts his attention to the guard again. "And you blocked his way?"

"He's not allowed in the main house unless it's time for him to return to his cell."

"Do you not see that this is an extenuating circumstance?"

"They could be faking it," he replies.

River arches a brow.

"I don't have time for this," I snap.

River's gaze shifts to me. "What's wrong with her?"

"She's feverish. I need to take her somewhere to cool her down so the fever drops. She passed out."

To his credit, he looks a bit fearful for his niece, though I imagine it has more to do with the fact that he needs her to do a job. "That is certainly problematic. Does she not have the medicine she needs?"

"Yes, but they are pills and, as you can see, she isn't awake to swallow them. Abana says there's a place I can take Bianca to cool her down. We need to do that."

"No one's allowed to leave this camp."

"I am asking you to give me permission. Send a guard with us if need be. Send ten. It's better than her dying, isn't it?" I'm frantic. I know it, he knows it. But I can't be bothered to care that he likely sees what I'm doing as begging. Honestly, I am.

He cocks his head to the side. "Fine. But I'm sending armed guards with you. Should you try and escape, they'll put a bullet in you. Understand?"

"Yes."

"You go with him, take one other," he tells the guard at the door.

"Yes, Sir."

He glances past me again. "Oh, and take the pregnant one and her husband with you, too," River adds. At my clearly confused expression, he adds, "Kill them first if they make any moves to escape."

"Here," Abana orders the guard. He pulls off to the side, then climbs out of the driver's side of the off-road vehicle, taking the keys with him. The second armed guard climbs off next, both of them remaining near the vehicle, ensuring they're not vulnerable to attack.

I can't even be bothered to care because Bianca still hasn't woken up, though the sounds she's making are terrifying. Groans every few minutes, her skin so slick with sweat that it's saturated her shirt, forcing it to cling to her like a second skin.

"This way." Abana, Idra, and Laring head toward the river, so I follow, my heart growing heavier with each and every step. Why is this happening? Why her?

I can't lose Bianca.

Not now.

Not ever.

I lost my parents.

My friends.

Brothers-in-arms.

My sister.

Is it my fate to lose her, too?

"Take her into the center. It's the deepest there," Abana orders. "Idra will need to go with you as the current is quite strong. He can help steady you both."

"Okay."

"Let me remove her shoes." Abana makes quick work of Bianca's shoes and socks, tossing them to the ground. "You go now."

Idra offers me a smile, then starts walking toward the river. He holds my elbow as I step down the bank and into the cool water. It pulls at my legs, the current stronger than it looks on the surface.

But it's cool.

Refreshing even.

Together, we move further into the river, stopping only once the water is up to our waists.

"Lower her slowly," Abana calls out. "To avoid shock."

I keep my gaze trained on her beautiful face as I slowly lower down into the water. Her feet hit it first, then I continue going down, almost losing my balance as the weight shifts. Idra keeps me rooted as I lower her further into the river, going slowly, just as Abana ordered.

Bianca barely reacts to the cooler water even as I finish submerging her up to her neck. I'm kneeling against the rocky bottom, but even though the stones bite into the flesh of my knees, I know I'd stay here for the rest of my life if it meant she'd wake.

"God," I whisper. "Please don't take her." I feel the plea all the way to my soul. It's unguarded, and even as stubborn as I've been, I know He has to be listening. "Take me. Please. She can help these people. She's been helping them. They need her."

Idra touches my shoulder and smiles knowingly at me, then he closes his eyes and bows his head.

Tears fill my eyes. I've been barely keeping it together over the past few weeks. Between being terrified about Eloise and how she's doing, to nearly dying, to forgiving yet still trying my best to keep Bianca at a distance, even though I know the love I carried for her all those years ago never actually went anywhere.

"God," I repeat. "I need her. Please don't take her too. Please, I'm—" The words get stuck in my throat. "She's the light guiding me back. I feel it every time I see her. It's like a spotlight that's slowly driving the darkness away. She's made me believe. Even though I'm far too stubborn to admit it. Please, God. I know You're there. I know You're good. And I know that You have a plan for everyone, but please—I'm begging You—don't let this be hers. Don't let it be mine." I close my eyes, and a tear falls.

I don't even know if I'm praying right, but as the words pour from my mouth, there's a sense of peace that settles over me. An unexplainable understanding that He is in charge even as I've done nothing but turn my back on Him.

"God, I know You're there. And I know You're in control."

Bianca groans, and I look down at her as her eyes flutter open. Emerald green with flecks of gold that have captured my every waking moment since we first met. "Hey," she chokes out.

"Thank you, God." I crush her against my chest, holding her to me.

"What's happening?" she asks.

"You passed out."

Her gaze clears, and it's as though I'm watching the fever disappear from her as we stand here in the cool water.

Idra grins widely at her, then squeezes my shoulder gently.

"Where are we?"

"A river," I reply. "Outside of the camp."

Her brow arches. But before she can respond, chaos breaks out on the embankment.

"Drop it!" someone orders. Realization stirs hope inside of me. I know that voice. Even before they come into view, I know that the cavalry has arrived. That God not only woke Bianca up, He brought us a rescue team.

Idra starts to move toward the bank where Laring and Abana stand, their hands raised. He looks back at me though, maintaining his hold on my shoulder as men pour from the trees. Four of them wearing baseball caps, tactical gear, bulletproof vests, and carrying rifles aimed directly at the two armed guards.

Three service dogs slip from the trees right alongside them, remaining silent, though I know without question that if given the order, the animals would lunge right into the action. They're highly trained, and my cousins never go anywhere without them.

"I said drop it!" the man orders again.

Keeping Bianca cradled against my chest, I make my way back to the embankment, moving as quickly as I can as Idra steadies the both of us.

I reach the edge and set Bianca down beside Abana while the men clear the area, disarming the guards and securing their wrists with zip ties. The man in charge turns toward me, and I find myself nearly weeping with joy as I stare into a familiar hazel gaze. "You know, Silas, one of these days I'm going to get tired of coming to your rescue."

I laugh—completely uncontrolled as I rush forward and embrace my cousin. "Bradyn, you have no idea how good it is to see you."

"I have a pretty good idea," he replies with a laugh. His gaze shifts past me. "Good to see you, too, Bianca."

"You too, Bradyn."

Michael comes rushing over next, his face shining with sweat. "See, and here we thought you guys were in danger, but instead you're over here taking an afternoon swim."

I hug my friend, then step back as he embraces Bianca.

"How did you know where to find us?" I ask.

"We've been camped outside the gates for about four days now, trying to find a way in. When we saw you come out, we figured this was as good a chance as any."

I raise my hand and wave at my youngest cousin, Tucker, who stays by the guards.

Glancing down at Bradyn's service dog, I offer the dog a smile. "Glad to see you got my message."

"Asking about Bravo was a smart move," Bradyn replies, patting the top of his dog's head. The animal looks up at him, tongue hanging out, complete adoration in his eyes.

"Thanks, Bravo," I tell the pup, who wags his tail. "How is Eloise? Is she okay?"

"She's good," Michael replies. "With Lance and Eliza. She's ready for you to come home though. We all are."

Bradyn's radio beeps.

"You get them? Over."

"Elijah?" I ask, recognizing the voice.

"We got 'em, over," Bradyn calls out. "Your buddy is showing Dylan a few tricks with the equipment."

"Elijah will do that." The weight of everything I'm carrying starts to lift just slightly. With them here, we stand a chance at freeing the people back at the camp, and we're no longer in this alone. I glance upward. Not that we ever really were.

Abana clears her throat, so I look back at her. "We need to return to the camp or they'll come looking for us."

"Go back?" Bradyn questions. "You don't have to go back."

"I cannot risk my people," she replies.

Idra begins speaking quickly, his tone panicked.

She responds to him, and his tone eases. "I told him that they do not have to return," she says to us. "Is that true?'

"Yes," Bradyn replies. "None of you do."

"I cannot leave my people behind," she repeats.

"You aren't," I reply, looking to Bianca. She reaches out and threads her fingers through mine, then squeezes my hand. I turn back to my cousin. "Who all's here? There's something we need to do before we go."

CHAPTER 24
Bianca

"Your vitals look great." Caleb offers me a smile as he uses hand sanitizer before helping me stand.

"Really?" I feel fine, but I'd honestly thought he'd find something wrong. Even if it was just a mild lingering fever. All the fatigue is gone, and I feel completely revitalized. As though I could do anything. Which, of course, medically speaking, makes no sense.

"Seriously, based on what you guys told me earlier, I would have thought you'd be seriously ill, but your fever is gone, your color is good, pulse is strong…it's like you were never sick."

"It's amazing," Abana whispers as she studies me. "You were truly ill."

"I feel fine now." I recall how I felt even when I woke up this morning, like my entire body was on fire. I'd barely managed to keep what little I ate at breakfast down.

"You're good now," Caleb replies. "And thank God for that."

"Thank God," I reply with a smile.

And then it hits me like a bright light straight into my heart. If I hadn't had the fever, we wouldn't have left the camp. We never would have been out here for the team to save us, and we wouldn't have the chance to save everyone else.

Thank you, God. I breathe a sigh of relief, the miracle settling around me. I turn to leave, and spot Silas standing just inside the medical tent. He's changed his clothes, wearing dark jeans and a white T-shirt that stretches over his expansive chest. His hair is dry now, his gaze piercing.

"We'll give you two just a minute." Caleb leaves the tent, Abana walking out with him. She pauses in the entryway and squeezes Silas's arm gently, then disappears outside.

He clears his throat. "How do you feel?"

"Good. Better. Caleb says it's like I wasn't even sick."

Silas nods. "Good."

There's an uncomfortable silence around us, something I can't quite put my finger on clinging to the very air we breathe. I scrape the still-damp hair off my neck and use the ponytail holder on my wrist to put it in a low bun. "How is Eloise? Caleb said Elijah was setting you up with a video conference so you could see her."

He smiles. "She's good. Looks like she's grown in the last three weeks."

"I bet she has."

"She told me she missed me and that she's ready for me to come home, but that it's okay if I can't yet because she's having so much fun with Eliza and Lance."

"That girl is mature beyond her years."

"You're telling me." He runs a hand over the back of his neck. "You're really okay?"

"I really am." I hesitate just a moment, unsure if I should speak my mind or not. Silas has never made it a secret that he's struggled with his belief, though after he nearly died I know he came around to the idea. To God. He's even prayed with me each night since. But is he truly open enough to hear my thoughts? Only one way to find out. After all, no one brought about change by remaining silent. So, I take a deep breath. "Look, I know you don't fully believe in it, but I can't help but feel like the fever was a tool to get us out. The fact that I was so sick earlier but now I'm totally fine? It shouldn't make sense."

His gaze levels on mine. "I prayed for you when we were in that water."

Silas's words stop me in my tracks. "You did?"

He nods. "I begged God not to take you too."

His tone is tortured, his expression strained. I reach for him, needing to bring him some sort of comfort. "Oh, Silas, I—"

At his expression, I drop my hand.

"I thought that I was being punished for the way I've been. See, I had the perfect family, Bianca. Loving parents, a supportive sister." He moves further into the room. "But I still felt like I needed more. My father wanted me to follow in his footsteps and run the ranch, but that just felt so torturous to me. I went into the military because I *wanted* more, and during my time in, I lost *everything*. My friends, my parents, the ranch, my sister—" He chokes on the last word, his grief still so fresh. "I couldn't help but wonder if it wasn't my punishment for not being content with what I had."

"Silas, I—"

He shakes his head, so I stop speaking. "And then this whole time we've been here. You've managed to remain so positive, behaving like a light to these people, speaking about God and the salvation He offered through the death of Jesus Christ, and all I could think was that I wish for one second I had the same type of blind faith you do." He moves in even closer, until he's standing only a few inches from me. "I got closer after this." He presses a hand over where the injury was. "But I still struggled, then when I was in that water with you, I *truly* prayed for what the first time since my sister died, and here you stand. Free of the chains that bound you back in that camp, and free of the sickness that plagued you only hours ago." Reaching up, he runs his hand over the side of my face.

I shiver at the touch, enjoying the contact far more than I should. Far more than is safe.

"It's enough to make a cynic like me understand that I don't know everything."

His words are everything to me.

His hope stoking the fire burning inside of me.

I tilt my face up to look at him, desperate for him to

take the next step even as I know it would change every-thing for the both of us.

His gaze drops to my lips, and he leans in.

I close my eyes.

My pulse thunders in response.

"Hey, there you guys are."

Silas pulls away from me like lightning struck him, and we both turn to Elijah, who's grinning like the idiot he so clearly is.

"Bad timing?" he jokes.

"What is it?" Silas demands.

"We thought you might want to come share your plan with us. As crazy as it might be." Michael grins. *Trou-blemaker*.

"We'll be right there," Silas replies, then turns back to me. "We're not done here."

"Good," I reply with a smile. 'Not done here' means there's more to come.

More that could possibly lead to everything I've wanted since I first laid eyes upon the SEAL.

———

"So you're telling me that you want to walk right back into the place you were just freed from?" Bradyn ques-tions, his arms crossed. He still looks exactly the same as he did the day he pulled Silas and me out of that jungle what feels like lifetimes ago.

While I don't know much about him, I do know that

he's the oldest of five brothers and the son of Silas's uncle. He also started the Hunt Brothers Search and Rescue Team after getting out of the Army, and since then he and his brothers have managed to track down people that were considered impossible to find.

I'm proof enough of that, given that twice now they've pulled me out of a nightmare.

"I think it's the only way we safely get everyone out," Silas replies.

Bradyn looks unconvinced. "How do you figure that?"

"River isn't going to kill us," Silas insists. "He needs us alive for whatever his goal is."

"We know his goal," Elijah replies. "He's working for Herman Bridges."

That's a name I never thought I'd hear again. "Yarrow's father?"

"One and the same," Elijah replies. "I had to do some digging, but it seems that River is in some deep water with the man."

"How so?" Silas questions.

"He owes him a quarter million dollars after a drug run River was hired to do got busted and the product confiscated," the second-youngest Hunt cousin, Dylan, responds.

"That's rough." Michael whistles.

"Tell me about it." Dylan walks over to the laptop on a table in the center of the tent, and a few seconds later a projector kicks on, painting the side of the tent in landscape photographs and maps. "According to our sources,

River assured Herman he could get him the money back—with interest—he just needed some extra time."

"Herman gave him two months," Elijah adds. "And time is almost up."

"They're here to get the diamonds, but they ran into an issue. The ground wasn't nearly as fertile as River was hoping for, and he's not even halfway to his goal yet."

"Until this morning," Dylan adds. "Our surveillance shows that a huge vein of diamonds was found just two hours ago."

"Which means they'll be gone soon," Caleb says.

"But not before killing every single person in that camp," Bradyn replies.

Both Silas and I whirl on him. "What do you mean?"

"Our comms also picked up communication from River, ordering the execution of every man, woman, and child in that camp as soon as the quota is met. They're leaving no witnesses."

My stomach churns, bile burning my throat as Bradyn speaks the words. I shouldn't be surprised. River is, after all, a murderer just like my father. But here I am, once again shocked at the level of evil twisting the hearts of some men. "We have to get back in there and stop him," I insist. "We have to get those people out."

"I agree," Silas replies.

"You do realize that if we can't get you out in time, those executions will extend to you too, right?" Michael asks.

"We'll get them out in time," Silas says.

But Bradyn, Elijah, Dylan, Caleb, Michael, Elliot, and Riley all look unconvinced. I imagine if Silas's other cousin Tucker was here, he'd likely have the same doubt stamped on his face.

"It's your mission," Bradyn says. "You tell us what you want us to do. We called for backup, but you should know it's not getting here anytime soon. Maybe forty-eight hours."

"We don't have that long," Silas insists.

"No," Bradyn agrees. "We don't."

Silas falls silent as he processes. We wait, they all die. We go in, there's a chance no one makes it out. Rock, meet hard place. *Lord, please guide us.*

"I'll sneak back in," Silas insists.

"How are you planning to explain the escape? How the three of you got away from the guards and Laring and Idra?"

"We're not going to get caught."

"No?"

"The guards are there to keep people from leaving, not keep us from getting back in. So I'll go in under the cover of night, sneaking through the camp and alerting the people there to the coming danger. You give me a weapon, and I'll take out some of the guards, making a path for them to escape to freedom."

I don't miss the fact that there are a lot of *I's* in Silas's plan. "I'm going with you."

He turns to me. "No."

"Yes. It's foolish for you to think you can do this alone. You need more boots on the ground."

"No one else can be risked," he insists.

"You forget I was a soldier, too," I snap, frustrated that he's planning a suicide mission like this when having me go in with him increases the odds of success.

"Bianca—"

"No. I go in too. We leave Abana, Laring, and Idra here where they're safe and go in together."

"I'm up for an adventure, I'll come in, too," Michael adds.

"Same," Bradyn replies.

"You can't all risk your lives like this. I have a better chance at getting in undetected if I go alone."

"And also a better chance at getting caught if no one is watching your six," Michael says. "You can't tell me you don't see the problem with this plan."

Silas's reaction is pure fear.

His earlier words come rushing back to me.

"*I lost* everything. *My friends, my parents, the ranch, my sister—*"

"Silas," I say, stepping forward and pressing my palm to his chest. "You're not going to lose us, but you will force us to lose you if you go in there alone. Please, we have to go as a team. A unit."

He closes his eyes and takes a deep breath. "We have to be quiet."

"And we will be," Bradyn replies. "We've all trained for this, cousin. You're not the only one."

Silas takes a deep breath and finally nods. "First, Bianca and I go in—but we're walking right through the gates."

Michael studies him. "And I'm forced to ask again, how do you plan on explaining your escape?"

"We'll distract River and the others while you get in and warn people," Silas replies. "With the attention on us, you stand a better chance at getting everyone out."

"Laring, Idra, and Abana?" I ask him.

"They stay here with Caleb. We may need medical help by the time this is over."

"You really think walking through the front gates is going to work?" Brady asks.

"I do," Silas replies. "Because with eyes on us, they won't be looking for you."

Brady claps his hands together. "Well, then, let's narrow down on some logistics and get this party started."

CHAPTER 25
Silas

"You look rough," Bianca says quietly as we make our way back toward the camp on foot. We'd had to change back into our dirty clothes, but at least they're mostly dry now.

"Yeah, I think Michael enjoyed taking some swings at me." I reach up and gently touch my sensitive cheekbone. I'd wanted him to make it look like we were attacked, so when I insist on talking only to River, it'll make it look that much more pertinent.

And the former boxer turned Army Ranger definitely delivered.

"Does it hurt?"

"Not the worst I've experienced," I reply. The truth is, the fear in my gut is a whole lot worse than the pain in my face. I'm terrified that this plan is going to fail. That in the failure, I'll lose everything that matters.

Bianca.

My cousins.

Michael.

Elijah.

My life—and therefore the chance to see Eloise grow up.

So many things at stake, and all because, once again, I can't allow myself to be freed while another is in chains. I think of that day I escaped the jungle. Of the calling I felt to save Bianca.

I feel the same thing now, only instead of one woman, it's an entire village of people far more deserving of freedom than I am.

"Listen." I stop walking. "If this goes sideways, I need you to promise me you'll save as many as you can—including yourself."

She tilts her face up to look at me, and the sun catches some bright strands in her otherwise dark hair. "Silas, it's all going to be fine."

"Please?"

She reaches up and cups my face, her hands running over a short beard courtesy of being unable to shave for three weeks. "We've been through a lot together, wouldn't you say?"

"That's an understatement."

"First, Lucian's compound, then tracking Michael, the hurricane, this—"

"What's your point?"

"My point is that we've survived it all."

"We can't live forever."

"No," she replies. "We can't."

I lean in, resting my forehead against hers. I want so badly to kiss her. To feel her lips on mine, but doing so when I'm not sure we'll even survive this feels wrong. It feels like a potential mistake that's just going to make it even harder for her to do what she needs to do, if leaving me behind is the only way to save herself.

"Can we pray?" I'm almost afraid to ask it, afraid that the request will sound foolish coming out of my mouth after all of the doubt over the past few weeks.

"We absolutely can," Bianca replies without hesitation.

"Can you do it? I'm still new to this."

Bianca smiles. "I am, too, but yes. I can. Dear Lord, we ask that You wrap us in Your protection as we walk back into the camp. Please guide us so that we may free those who are being held there, and so that we can make it back home safely. Please work through us, Lord, and let Your will be done. Amen."

"Amen," I repeat.

"Amen, brother," Michael, Elijah, and my cousins all say in tandem through the earpiece I'm wearing.

A lump in my throat makes it almost impossible to breathe, but as I pull away, I linger near Bianca for just a moment. "I need you to survive," I tell her.

"I need you to survive," she repeats. "We have unfinished business, Williamson."

Chuckling, I pull away. "You're not wrong there." Straightening, I face the direction of the camp. We're close, only about a quarter mile away, but the sun has already sunk on the horizon, and with each passing moment, it gets darker and darker. Which will be great for Bradyn and the others to sneak in, but not so good for us walking along the barren road. "Let's do this."

We begin walking again, and I think back to the last time I saw my cousins. It was at Sierra's funeral. They'd driven in from the family ranch. While Bradyn and Dylan had gone back right after to tend to their brand-new business, Elliot, Riley, and Tucker stayed behind to help me go through Sierra and her husband's things.

They'd helped me with Eloise those first few weeks, and without them, I'm not sure I would've survived the grief that threatened to drown me. They'd spoken of God to me then, too, all of them believers.

But I'd ignored them, choosing instead to wallow in my own anger.

How many years did I spend as a bitter man, hellbent on living my life in misery because I felt I didn't deserve any joy? Even the happiness I've found watching Eloise grow filled me with guilt because my sister was missing so many milestones in her daughter's life.

Will my cousins suffer the same fate as her tonight?

Or will they survive?

What about Michael? With Reyna back home, he's likely going to be starting a family soon. What if he doesn't get the chance? What about Elijah? What if he never gets to return to Andie and she's forced to bury another loved one?

As though she can sense my panic, Bianca reaches

down and threads her fingers through mine. When I look at her, she smiles, and a sense of peace settles over me.

It's going to be okay.

It has to be okay.

"Stop right there!"

Both Bianca and I freeze. She pulls her hand from mine and puts both up in the air. I do the same as two of River's guards come rushing toward us, the tactical lights at the end of their weapons blinding.

"What are you doing out here? Where's your detail?"

"Gone," I reply. "And I can't say anything else until I speak to River."

My cousin Dylan is recording everything that's said, and with any luck, we'll not only free the imprisoned, but we'll also have enough evidence to put River Culvers away for good.

If we survive, that is.

"You'll tell us what we want to know," the guard says, then slams the butt of his rifle into my stomach. I groan, bile burning me from the inside.

"Stop it!" Bianca yells.

"You have no say. Tell us where your detail is," he growled. "Or you're next. Woman or not, makes no difference to me."

I step in front of her, my stomach still burning. "You won't lay a finger on her. And as for your buddies? They're likely rotting away in some enemy camp right now."

"What do you mean, enemy camp?"

"Look at my face," I say, pointing to the bruises courtesy of Michael.

"You're welcome," he says in my ear.

"We didn't all make it back," I repeat. "Now, I want to speak with River."

The guard narrows his gaze on me but grabs me by the arm and yanks me forward. The second one grips Bianca's arm and tugs her too. Her gaze briefly finds mine, but then we both focus straight ahead as we're escorted back through the large metal gates.

The area's empty, though that's to be expected given the lateness of the hour. Curfew has likely been enacted already, and anyone out would be subject to River's brand of questioning.

The guards lead us toward the house and up the porch steps. One raises his fist and knocks on the door. A few seconds pass in silence before it's opened, and Yarrow is standing on the other side, a massive grin on his face. "Just in time!" he exclaims, then grabs Bianca and pulls her into the house.

I'm shoved in from behind, barely managing to catch my footing to keep from falling over.

Yarrow tugs Bianca through the house, his mood so vastly different than typical that it sets my nerves on edge. What changed? Is it that they met their quota? I think back to the empty streets.

Is it possible we're too late?

He pulls her into the dining room, and she gasps, then tries to step backward. He wraps an arm around her throat and keeps her exactly where she stands. I rush forward, only to have the cool barrel of a pistol pressed to the back of my neck.

"I'd slow down if I were you," a voice I don't recognize says. "Wouldn't want to spoil the fun just yet, would we? Move."

I do as he says and continue forward, stopping right beside Bianca.

River's tied to a chair directly across from us, his chest covered in blood, while a man to his right eats dinner. River is clearly dead, but hasn't been for long as the blood is still wet on his chest.

The man wipes his mouth with a fabric napkin, then turns to face us—and smiles.

The recognition is instant because he's the older version of Yarrow. A man with the same features, the same darkness in his gaze. Only less wild. The father is calculated while the son is rash.

"Well, well, well, what have we here?" he asks, fully facing us.

"This is my fiancée, father," Yarrow says. "Selena Culvers."

"Selena Culvers. She's a bit dirty, but a looker."

I start to step forward, but the man behind me tugs me back. Herman shifts his gaze to me. "And who are you?"

"The SEAL," Yarrow replies, clearly disgusted.

"A big boy, aren't you? Tall. Filled out. Want a job? I could use a new head of the Culvers organization. More of a management position, really. You can even keep her." He gestures to Bianca. "My gift to you since, from what I hear, you're fond of her."

"I'll pass," I snap. "Why did you kill him?"

"His usefulness ran out," Herman replies. "The question is, where were you two?"

"Bianca had a fever, I took her to a spring to cool her down."

"And who is Bianca?"

"Me," she replies.

"I thought your name was Selena." He looks from her to his son.

"She changed her name," Yarrow explains. "But I prefer Selena." He presses a noisy kiss to her temple, and I lunge forward again.

Pain explodes in the back of my head as I'm brought to my knees, the barrel of the gun now pressed against my temple. "I told you to remain where you were," the man orders.

I look up at him now. He's tall, likely nearly as tall as I am, his hair bleached white, his dark eyes near black. He looks like a loose cannon, like a man who enjoys causing pain. Something I recognize because River had the same look in his eye as he tortured me all those years ago.

"Easy there, Frank, we can't be killing him just yet. He might prove useful." Herman stands, and the maid we haven't seen since our first night here rushes in to collect his plate. She's careful to not look at River's body, though her complexion is incredibly pale.

"It's true," Yarrow says. "She was sick. I looked into it myself."

"I'm sure she was." The way Herman eyes Bianca makes my skin crawl. I want to rewind time and force her to stay back at camp.

Lord, if You're listening, please help us. Please keep me strong so I can save them.

"The question is," Herman says, "what to do with you both."

"Do *not* harm Selena," Yarrow replies. "She's my fiancée. And he *can't* have her."

"You don't need to marry a Culvers anymore, Yarrow. They're trash. They always have been."

"Not this one," he replies. "She's mine. I want to keep her."

He's talking about her like she's a toy. An animal to be kept in captivity. The shift in Yarrow's personality is so vast, it's hard to even comprehend that this is the same man who was River's number two, when right now he's behaving like a spoiled and incompetent child.

"We'll discuss it later. That one needs to be put down if he's not going to help, though." He points to me. "I can see that he'll be trouble."

"I'll do it," Yarrow offers with a gleeful smile. "Happily."

"No."

"You don't get to speak," Yarrow tells Bianca, crushing her back against his chest.

"We're moving into place," Michael says through the earpiece. "Stay alive a bit longer."

"Nearly there," Bradyn confirms. "How are the charges?"

"Set and armed," Elijah replies.

As they converse in my ear, I do my best to hide my excitement. This will all be over in mere minutes.

We just have to survive for a short period of time, and then we'll be done.

"Hold her," Yarrow tells the man he called Frank. He hesitates a second, but Herman nods, so Frank grabs Bianca by the arm. Yarrow releases her as I get to my feet. "River believed you were an untamable force," he tells me. "The man thought you had the strength of ten and the willpower of twice that."

"What a nice compliment," I sneer.

"I see you for what you are though. Weak. Pathetic. A coward trying too hard to play hero. Hold him."

Two men grip my arms. "You seem awfully worried for a man who believes me to be a coward."

"Yarrow, don't," Bianca pleads. "Leave him be."

"He doesn't have it in him to do anything," I tell her, though I keep my gaze trained firmly on Yarrow. I'll take his anger. His wrath. Because I'm strong enough to do both. After all, I am the distraction.

He slams his fist into my gut. The pain shoots straight through me, but aside from a small grunt, I do what I can to hide it.

"Is that all?" I ask.

Yarrow hits me again, this time striking my face. "How's that feel, SEAL? Strong man?"

Warmth trickles from my lip. I smile through it. Never in my life have I felt such calmness in the face of a storm. Such peace in the midst of what should be fear. Is this what faith is? Knowing that my fate is in the hands of the One who created everything? And if that's so, what do I have to fear?

Yarrow hits me again.

Again.

Striking me with such ferocity I can feel his growing anger with each and every blow. Bianca begs for him to stop, but I say nothing.

I take my licks. Letting each of them connect because soon—

"Fire in the hole!" Bradyn yells in my ear.

Boom.

The explosion rocks the house we're in.

Windows shatter, and Yarrow pales. "What was that?" he demands, turning toward his father, who's staring at me with palpable rage.

"Ask your friend."

Yarrow whirls on me. "What was that?" he demands again.

I meet his gaze, even though my vision is a bit blurry from the hits, and smile. "The cavalry."

CHAPTER 26
Bianca

"We have to get you out of here," Frank yells to Herman as he leaves me and rushes around to grab his boss.

"Let's go, Yarrow," Herman orders. "Leave them!"

"No! I'm not leaving things unfinished!" Yarrow screams, then slams his fist into Silas's gut. He withdraws his weapon, and I sprint forward, slamming my body into him. He goes down with the force of my hit, and pain shoots through my shoulder, straight up into my neck. "No!" he yells, rearing back his fist.

I prepare for the hit, but seconds later, he's ripped off of me and flung across the room. Silas comes into view above me.

"Are you okay?" He reaches for me, pulling me to my feet.

"I think I dislocated my shoulder." I cradle my arm

against my body, the pain familiar, but that doesn't make it any easier to bear. "Otherwise, I'm okay."

"Want me to reset it?"

I groan. "Yes."

He grips my arm. "Breathe."

I do.

He slams it back into its socket and I scream, my head falling back as my body jerks. But the seconds tick by and the pain resides, becoming a bearable ache. An ache I can deal with, but trying to run with a dislocated shoulder? Not good.

"Don't move!"

Silas stops and turns toward Yarrow, who's holding a grenade in his hand. Terror ices the pain as I stare what could very well be my death straight in the face.

"You had a job to do," Yarrow snarls, his eyes wide and wild. "And you failed. It's okay though. I was going to kill you when I was done playing with you anyway."

At one point, Yarrow served as my own personal nightmare. A boy I'd trusted who'd tried to force himself on me, then laid on the floor, promising to do terrible things to me should he ever see me again. I think I'd built him up in my mind over the years, telling myself he was far more terrifying than he actually was.

"You don't have to do this," I tell him, putting up both hands. "It's not too late for you to come around."

"Come around?" he spits out. "I'm not the one who needs to come around, *Selena.* You were born into this life, and you thought you could escape. Who's the delusional one?"

"We can't choose where we're born," I tell him. "But we can choose to stay in or leave. I wanted a different life."

"You had a life! A job to do!" he screams.

Outside, people scream. Chaos reigns.

Silas moves in front of me. "You want to take out your anger on me? Fine. But you leave Bianca out of it."

"Her name is Selena!" Yarrow snaps, ripping the grenade's pin free.

"You're making a mistake!" Silas bellows, frantic now. If Yarrow drops that grenade—we won't make it out of the house in time.

"No. I'm making a choice. If I can't have her, no one can." He throws the grenade then turns and sprints from the room.

Silas looks to me for a split second, and in that moment, everything around us slows to a near stop. His eyes fill and he smiles. "Run," he says, then throws himself onto the grenade.

"No!" I scream. I hesitate, too afraid to move and not wanting to live without him. A second passes, then two, as I wait for the moment when everything I love will be robbed from me.

But nothing happens.

Silas sits up, eyeing the grenade warily as he pushes off the floor and rushes toward me. He grabs my good hand and tugs me out of the room. We're just stepping foot outside when the grenade goes off.

It collapses the house behind us, and we're thrown forward—away from the blast.

Debris rains down on us. My ears are ringing, the pain in my shoulder spreading through the entire side of my body, but as I sit here, staring at the house we were *just* standing in, I'm hit with the overwhelming love of the God who kept us safe.

I turn toward Silas sitting beside me, his face covered in ash. He's staring straight ahead, shocked, confused—but then he turns to me and grins. "He saved us," he calls out, the words barely audible with the still fading ringing in my ears.

"Yes," I call back. "He did."

Silas cups the back of my head and yanks me toward him, slamming his mouth onto mine. He kisses me like the world is ending and we're out of time. Everything I've ever wanted, ever craved, comes slamming into me in one moment, along with the understanding that he was made for me, and I for him.

Silas Williamson is the only man I've ever really loved.

And until the day I die, he'll be my forever.

However long we have.

"Okay, you two. I know you nearly got blown up, but you can't expect us to do all the work." Michael drops to the ground beside Silas as we pull apart.

"All the work?" Silas replies. "You get Herman?"

"And Yarrow. It sounded like River was dead through the earpiece, but we haven't been able to confirm it."

"Consider it confirmed," Silas replies, then gestures

toward the house. "He was in there and was dead before it blew up."

"Okay. I'll let Bradyn know."

"The people?" I ask. "Are they okay?"

Michael smiles and nods. "They're fine. We found a man to translate and pulled them all out once the guards were subdued. Look." He points to the right, so I turn my attention over there, and emotion turns me into a puddle of joy as I see the men, women, and children dancing down the street.

They smile.

Laugh.

All of them free from the shackles River had placed upon them.

Silas lies back down on the ground, and I lie down beside him, taking his hand in mine.

"All right, I get it. I'm a third wheel." Michael pushes up from the ground. "Five minutes though, guys. We have work still to do. And like I said, I'm not doing it all."

I turn my face to Silas, surprised to find him already looking at me. "What is it?" I ask, cheeks heating.

"Just wondering how I ever survived without you."

By the time day breaks, the guards, Yarrow, and Herman are all on their way toward an airplane hangar, about to board a flight that will take them back to the States and a trial that will land them in prison.

Apparently, one of Bradyn's buddies at the FBI has been trying to nail River and Herman for years now, and we just handed him every bit of evidence he needs.

I stare down at the worn Bible that I pulled out of the medical building earlier and smile. God came through for us, just as He always does. But even though Silas and I just faced down the evilness of Yarrow and his father, I feel lighter than before. Exhausted, yet exhilarated.

Today, we'll be heading home. In a few hours, Silas and I will be on a private plane, heading back to the small airport just outside of Hope Springs. He'll get to see Eloise, and I'll get to return to my home.

To my life.

Only this time, it'll be even better than before. I smile at Silas when he turns toward me. Warmth spreads through my belly when he grins back. The darkness that's been in his gaze ever since I saw him again is gone, leaving behind the bright light that he'd been for me when we'd been wandering through that jungle, barely surviving.

Abana steps up beside me. "You saved us."

"I told you I would free you."

"You did," Abana replies. "But not all people keep their promises. You did."

"I want you to have this." I hold out the Bible, and she takes it.

"Are you certain?"

"I am."

She smiles. "You gave us hope, Bianca. For that, we will be eternally grateful."

"I didn't do anything," I tell her. "God did. He deserves your praise, not me."

She smiles again. "We will continue to read this Bible."

"Good." My gaze finds Silas again.

"Ah, yes. You two belong together. Soul bound, as I would call it," she says. "I am happy that you worked through whatever was between you." When I turn to look at her, she adds, "It was easy enough to see."

I laugh. "Things are definitely different."

Abana loops her arm through mine. "But better."

I nod. "Much, much better."

CHAPTER 27
Silas

TWO DAYS LATER

Showered, and wearing fresh clothes, I step up to the front door of Lance and Eliza's house, my stomach a pit of nerves. It's been nearly a month since I saw Eloise. And even though we video chatted and spoke on the phone, I'm still terrified she's not going to want me back.

What if she's grown so fond of Eliza and Lance that she doesn't want to come home?

The door opens and Eliza rushes forward and throws her arms around me. "You're back! Eloise! He's here!" She tugs me into the house, and Eloise comes around the corner.

Her beautiful little face turns red, and her eyes fill with tears as she races toward me. "Uncle Lassy!"

I drop to the floor, catching her as she throws both arms around my neck. My body still aches from the beating I took first from Yarrow, then the explosion, but it's worth every second of pain.

My throat tightens, tears burning in my eyes as I hold on to the little girl that may not be mine by birth but is mine in every other way. My sweet girl. My life.

"Nugget, I missed you so much."

"I missed you, Uncle Lassy. I thought you might not come back."

"Nugget, I will always come back for you." I pull her away just enough that I can cup her little face and brush the tears from her cheeks. "I love you so much, honey."

"I love you, too." She beams at me, then her gaze turns serious. "What happened to your face?"

I laugh, recalling just how rough I looked in the mirror this morning—bruises, cuts, one eye bloodshot. "I had a bit of an accident. But I'm okay."

"You're sure?"

"Yes, Nugget. I'm okay now."

Lance comes out of the hall and smiles at me as he wraps an arm around Eliza's shoulders. "It's good to see you, brother."

"You, too. You know," I say to Eloise, "I brought someone else too." Bianca steps into the house wearing a yellow sundress with small white daisies all over the fabric. Her dark hair is down and loose around her face, her smile bright.

"Bianca!" Eloise yells, then wiggles herself out of my grip.

Bianca kneels just in time to catch the excited Eloise as

she throws her arms around her. "I missed you so much, kid."

"I missed you too! You were gone for so long."

"I know."

"Guess what?"

"What?"

"We had another storm! Not as bad as before, but it was scary, and I remember your roof fell in, but we went and checked, and it was okay."

Bianca beams. "Thank you. I'm not even sure how to repay you for being so awesome."

"You can come color with me later."

"Done."

With Eloise giving Bianca attention, I shift mine to Lance. "Can we talk?"

"Of course." Lance kisses Eliza on the side of her head and walks down the hall into his office. I follow, shutting the door softly behind me. "Is everything all right?"

"A lot happened to me when I was over there. A lot changed."

"Bianca?"

"Yes." My cheeks heat. "That relationship is still new, but that's one of them."

"What else?"

"I found God," I tell him, unsure how else to put it. The statement feels so simple, yet the power it carries is stronger than anything I've ever felt.

Lance's expression turns absolutely thrilled, his smile brilliant. His own eyes fill. "Welcome home, brother."

My heart warms. "It's strange that I found Him there, in that pit. But I did. Bianca helped. She talked about God, about His word and His promises, but when I thought we were done for, He was there. Bringing us out of the darkness."

"As He always does."

"Then there was the grenade—" I start.

"Grenade? I haven't been fully briefed on what happened," he adds.

"Yarrow Bridges threw a grenade at us, and all I could think about was Bianca. I threw myself on it, ready to take that blow if it meant she walked away, but it didn't go off."

"Dud?"

I shake my head. "It exploded the second we were outside. It shouldn't have been that long of a delay. There's no logical reason why it didn't kill me. The only thing that makes sense to me is that God had a reason for saving me again, and I want to use what's left of my life, this second chance, to honor Him in every way I possibly can."

"Again? How many times did you nearly die over there?"

"Twice," I reply. "But I think He was there that first time, too."

"What do you mean?"

"This might sound crazy, but I keep thinking about that man who saved me when Lucian had me. How he was just there, and I never saw him again. He told me that I had more to do in this life. Do you think it might be possible—"

"That God sent someone to set you free? Brother, we need to do a Bible study." Lance reaches out and grips my shoulder. "That's amazing."

"I have some significant savings left over from my time in the service, along with the inheritance I received after my parents passed. I already spoke to Pastor Redding, but I want to use it to build a church in that village. They're rebuilding everything River destroyed, and I want to contribute. He's going to talk to some of his friends and see if he can get an assistant pastor to come preach here, so we can go back, and he can help me get everything set up."

"Silas, that's amazing."

I swallow hard, surprised that I'm far more nervous than I realized. "I'll need time off. I know it will put a strain on the company, but I feel like I *need* to help them. As though it's what I'm supposed to do."

He smiles. "Don't even worry about it," he replies. "We've got it covered. Spreading The Word is bigger than what we do."

Relief floods my system even as I'm possibly more nervous about what I'm going to ask next. "That's not all, either. Listen, I know that I'm asking a lot of you already, but I'd like for you and Eliza to be Eloise's godparents. I'm having her baptized Sunday."

Lance's eyes glisten with emotion. "Brother, we'd be honored."

"There's still more."

He doesn't even hesitate. "Then lay it on me. Anything you need."

"I want to be baptized in the same river I first felt Him. Pastor Redding has agreed to baptize me when we return to that village in a couple of months. I want you there with me. If you're willing. I know it's asking a lot. I'm going to take Eloise too, I—"

"It's not asking a lot, and I would love to be there. I will be there." Lance wraps his arms around me and pulls me in for a crushing hug. "You have no idea how happy I am, Silas. How proud I am that you've found your faith."

"I am too," I reply as I pull away. "I know it's going to take time to fully understand what it all means, but I know that I was saved for a reason. That there's a purpose to my life and even if it's not completely clear yet, it will be."

"Amen to that, brother. Amen to that."

It's been weeks since I last cooked, and it feels nice to be back in the kitchen. I was never one for elaborate meals, but tonight I'm determined to make it special. Eloise is coloring at the dining room table, singing happily along with the Christian playlist coming through the speakers.

I finish blending the mashed potatoes, then check the broccoli roasting in the oven, before stepping out onto the back porch to check the steaks I put on the grill.

Bianca's standing on her porch, staring out at the

ocean, her eyes closed, face tilted up toward the dimming sky.

She's so beautiful.

So breathtaking.

The light that guided me home.

"You're stunning."

She turns toward me. "You're not so bad yourself. I was just about to head over. I wanted to take a moment to pray though."

I leave the grill and head toward the barrier between us and hold out my arms. "Come on, then."

She arches a brow. "You're going to lift me?"

"I won't let you fall. Don't you trust me?"

She crosses toward me, her feet bare against the wooden floor of the deck. "With everything that I am." Raising her arms, she wraps them around my neck and lifts her legs. I pull her against me and turn, lifting her over the short railing between us.

But once I have her in my arms, I don't want to let her go.

I drop my face and kiss her, pressing my lips to her soft mouth. The kiss is a promise. A slow, delicate dance that expresses how much I vow to cherish her. For the rest of my life.

"Marry me," I whisper when I pull away.

"What?"

"Marry me."

"If I say no will you still put me down?"

"I don't know," I reply. "Maybe."

She grins. "I will marry you, Silas Williamson."

"I don't have a ring yet. But I'll get one."

"I'll marry you with or without one. You're all I want, Silas. All I've ever wanted."

I kiss her again, then spin in a slow circle before setting her down. It's strange that less than a month ago, I was closed off, terrified of the feelings I couldn't shake when it came to this woman.

I was still grieving, pained by the losses I've suffered over the years.

But now, I don't know, I feel like I can start to move forward with the life granted to me when I didn't die back in that jungle all those years ago.

"Bianca! You're here!" Eloise comes rushing out and grips Bianca's hand. "Come color!"

Bianca offers me a final smile, her cheeks flushed pink, as she follows Eloise into the house. I watch as she sits on a chair beside my little girl and starts happily chatting as she chooses a crayon.

This is my life.

Forever.

Always.

And I'm finally able to *see* the blessings God gave me even when I was determined to keep my face turned from Him.

Bianca

THREE MONTHS LATER

S tanding on what used to be a desolate street but is now a bustling village makes my heart far happier than I ever thought possible. Standing here holding Eloise's hand, while Silas shakes the hand of this town's new pastor—well—it makes it that much sweeter.

"Abana!" Eloise calls out.

Abana looks over and smiles widely, then holds her arms out as Eloise goes rushing for her. We've been here for a month now, and Eloise fits right in with all of the other children. She's part of their family now, just as we are.

I cross over toward Abana.

"Good day?" she asks as she releases Eloise and straightens.

"Great day," I reply.

"I agree." Abana raises her hand in greeting as Laring, new baby in tow, steps out of the small cottage built just for her and Idra. Everyone here pitched in over the past few months and got most of the village built back better than it was before.

And now that the villagers get to profit off the diamonds found in the mine, they're flourishing. The church was finished within a month, the wooden building complete with cushioned pews and a cross built and brought here by Silas's cousin, Bradyn, who as it turns out, loves working with his hands.

It seems so surreal that not that long ago, we were standing amongst pure destruction, and now all around us, people are happily living their lives, laughing, playing, and selling goods they crafted or food they grew.

A hand slips into mine so I tilt my face up to look at Silas. He smiles down at me. "You ready?"

"I am. Are you?" I ask.

He nods. "More than. I feel like I've been waiting for this moment my entire life."

"Then let's do it."

He leans down and presses his lips to mine. Lance and Pastor Redding make their way over to us, both men chatting happily. Pastor Redding has been in his element since we arrived, along with a friend of his who is going to build a seminary over here in addition to being a guest pastor himself.

"You ready?" Pastor Redding asks Silas.

"I am. Eloise!" he calls out.

She gives Adara a high five, then rushes over toward

us. Silas lifts her up and sets her on his shoulders. "Let's go do this."

We all climb into the back of trucks, and they take off down the dirt road, heading past where River's gates once stood, and out into the lush wilderness. I close my eyes and smile as the warm wind hits my face.

I'm so at peace. So completely and utterly different from where I was even a year ago.

Lord, thank You for this moment. For this time here, in this lovely place. Please watch over these people and guide them further into Your light. Please watch over Silas as well. Please continue to work in his life, growing his faith into abundance. In Jesus' name I pray. Amen.

I open my eyes as we park near the river Silas took me to when I'd been sick. The same place we were rescued by Michael, Bradyn, and his team.

Silas climbs out first, taking Eloise with him before reaching up for me.

"Come stand with me, baby girl," Adara says as she takes Eloise's hand and guides her over toward the riverbank where Laring and Idra are already waiting.

Pastor Redding falls into step beside us, and together, alongside Lance, we head down toward the river, too. The water is bright and clear, the air around us charged with the hope we found in this very same place three months ago.

Pastor Redding heads into the water, and Lance follows.

Silas takes my hand and together, we walk down into the water.

It's cool around my ankles, wrapping the fabric of my skirt around my legs. My heart is pounding, my soul warm even before we make it to the very center where Pastor Redding and Lance are waiting.

I turn back toward the bank.

Michael and Reyna are waiting there, along with Andie and Elijah. Bradyn, Elliot, and Riley are also present, standing on the bank with matching smiles as they watch their cousin prepare to officially accept Jesus.

I take a deep breath.

Pastor Redding begins speaking. "Let us pray." We all bow our heads. "Dear Lord, we thank You for every blessing You have bestowed upon us. Thank You for the salvation through Your death and resurrection. We ask that You be with Silas and Bianca as they take the next steps in their faith, and that You guide them so that their faith is ever-growing. In Jesus' name we pray, amen."

"Amen," I whisper at the same time Silas does.

"Baptism is a time of renewal. Of accepting Jesus and agreeing to follow Him in every part of your life. You are washing away the old and becoming reborn in Him. Silas, do you accept Jesus as your Lord and Savior, and recognize that He is our salvation?"

"I do," Silas replies. He releases my hand as Lance takes one of his arms and Pastor Redding takes the other. Silas kneels into the water and leans back.

"I baptize you in the name of the Father, and of the Son,

and of the Holy Spirit." Pastor Redding dips Silas back into the water with Lance helping to keep hold of him. He comes up out of the water with a wide smile, water slicking his hair back and clinging to his clothes.

"Congratulations, brother," Lance says, wrapping his arms around Silas.

Pastor Redding pulls Silas in for a hug too. "I'm proud of you. Welcome to the family," he says with a wide, proud smile.

Tears fill my eyes as Silas turns to me, his joy radiating from him.

He steps to the side so I can get near Pastor Redding. Lance takes hold of my arm while Pastor Redding loops his arm through mine, just as he did Silas.

"Bianca, do you accept Jesus as your Lord and Savior, and recognize that He is our salvation?"

"Absolutely."

"Then I baptize you in the name of the Father, and of the Son, and of the Holy Spirit," he says, then dips me back into the water. It closes around me, enveloping my body. As I break the water, I feel a warmth spread through my chest, a peace that settles around me like a familiar blanket.

"Congratulations, Bianca." Pastor Redding pulls me in for a hug. "You do not carry your burdens alone, child," he says to me. "You can rest now."

The tears break through, and I wrap my arms around him again, hugging him tightly.

Cheers erupt from the embankment as I pull away, hug

Lance, and throw myself into Silas's arms. He hugs me tightly, holding me against him.

$$\mathcal{S}ilas$$

There is nothing that this life can throw at me that will drown me. Not with God on my side. Sure, I'll still experience tough times driven by loss, grief, and pain. But there will never be a moment where we are forsaken. Only molded into a powerful servant of Christ.

What a gift that is, to be loved by Him.

To be given the chance to love and be loved.

The water rushes around us, and I glance over at Bianca, who's smiling widely. Soon, she'll be my wife. Eloise will—God willing—become a big sister, as we both want children.

I'll still help others through Knight Security, and plan to fly here one month a year to volunteer, doing whatever it is they need. I feel drawn to this place, to these people.

Things have never been so clear as they are to me now. I have a purpose. A plan.

And I'll follow Jesus wherever He leads me.

I didn't find my faith in a church pew on a sunny Sunday morning. Not that there's anything wrong with that, of course, it's just not how it worked for me.

No, I found mine walking through a fiery furnace, feeling like I was going to lose everything. But just like Shadrach, Meshach, and Abednego, I was not burned by the flames.

I was saved.

Because even though I felt alone, I wasn't. God was with me, shielding me from the flames just as He has done my entire life.

I was too stubborn to see it, too blinded by pain and burdened by what I thought I knew rather than the truth that was always in front of me.

He brought me out of the jungle.

He brought me home to Eloise.

He brought me Bianca.

And through Jesus, I found my salvation.

WHAT A RIDE! I HAVE LOVED EVERY SINGLE MOMENT OF this series, and I am so grateful you came along on this journey with me! As you probably guessed, there's more to come! I am so thrilled to announce that my next series, Hunt Brothers Search and Rescue, is debuting soon with Bradyn's story! So if you loved meeting Silas's cousins, then get ready for another adventure! This time, with former Army Rangers turned Texas Cowboys.

(Be sure to click here or subscribe to my newsletter via the QR code on the Pictures of Hope page, so that you can read the first three chapters for FREE when they become available!)

COMING SOON...

A VETERAN WITH A HEART OF GOLD AND THE WOMAN HE NEVER SAW COMING.

Former Special Forces Operative Bradyn Hunt may have traded a battlefield for his family's ranch in Texas, but that doesn't mean he stopped fighting.

As the founder of Hunt Brother's Search & Rescue, he and his team take on missing persons cases that no one else can solve. They've retrieved people from the very depths of hell-on-earth, which is bound to leave some scars. And he certainly carries his fair share of them.

Kennedy Smith has had many names and lived many different lives. Running from her past, her only goal is to survive long enough to see the next sunrise. Her most recent identity is as a ranch hand in a small North Texas town.

Run by Army veterans, she figures there's no better place to hide than the Hunt family ranch. That is, until she begins to grow attached to the eldest Hunt brother, Bradyn. She should run. After all, not getting attached is rule number one to staying alive. But before she can bring herself to leave, the threat shows up on her doorstep, dragging Bradyn right into the flames alongside her.

Bradyn has saved the lives of hundreds of people, but can he protect Kennedy from the ghosts of her past? Or will her secrets burn everything he's built to the ground?

If you're looking for a swoony romantic suspense with a

protective hero who lives by faith, a team of brothers who follow God, and a woman fighting to survive, then BRAVO is just what you're looking for!

This Christian Romantic Suspense deals with:
-Coping with trauma
-Discovering your worth
-Seeking God in everything
-Healing from your past

The Hunt Brother's Search & Rescue series can be enjoyed in any order, though the suggested reading order is:
Hunt Brothers Search & Rescue: BRAVO
Hunt Brothers Search & Rescue: ECHO
Hunt Brothers Search & Rescue: ROMEO
Hunt Brothers Search & Rescue: DELTA
Hunt Brothers Search & Rescue: TANGO

Acknowledgments

Every single morning I wake up, I offer God thanks for bringing me into another day. I pray that He will guide me through every waking moment, and show my family and me what we can do to glorify Him.

Without Him, I would not be here, and I certainly would not have the love of storytelling that I do. I cannot offer enough thanks to God, because without Him none of this would be possible.

I want to thank my husband, Nathan, who has been my biggest supporter since the very beginning of my career back in 2016. There has never been a moment where he hesitated to offer me support, encouragement, and it is because of his selfless love that I am the woman I am today. He is my partner, my love, the father of my children, and my absolute best friend.

To my lovely children who are my greatest blessings in this life. To Brenna, who is in the process of reading these books and makes me so beyond excited to write more because she tells me constantly how much she loves them. To Ayden, who encourages me with her wonderful hugs and bright smiles. To Declan, who is always right there to offer me a hug and a kiss on the cheek. You three have no idea how much your dad and I love you, and how incredibly proud we are to be your parents!

To my editing team, HEA Author Services. Thank you for making my words shine!

To my proofers, Dawn and Tasha, you ladies are beyond appreciated!

To my ARC team who have come through with wonderful reviews.

To my Coastal Hope group, and the wonderful readers in there.

And to you.

Thank you for reading and for loving these characters just like I do.

Scriptures used in this series are:

Pages of Promise

"This is my command—be strong and courageous! Do not be afraid or discouraged. For the Lord your God is with you wherever you go." Joshua 1:9

Searching for Peace

"This is the message we heard from Jesus and now declare to you: God is light, and there is no darkness in him at all. So we are lying if we say we have fellowship with God but go on living in spiritual darkness; we are not practicing the truth. But if we are living in the light, as God is in the light, then we have fellowship with each other, and the blood of Jesus, his Son, cleanses us from all sin. If we claim we have no sin, we are only fooling ourselves and not living in the truth. But if we confess our sins to him, he is faithful and just to forgive us our sins and to cleanse us from all wickedness." 1 John 1:5-9

"A peaceful heart leads to a healthy body; jealousy is like cancer in the bones." -Proverbs 14:30

Second Chance Serenity

"Bless those who persecute you. Don't curse them; pray that God will bless them. Be happy with those who are happy, and weep with those who weep. Live in harmony with each other. Don't be too proud to enjoy the company of ordinary people. And don't think you know it all! Never pay back evil with more evil. Do things in such a way that everyone can see you are honorable. Do all that you can to live in peace with everyone. Dear friends, never take revenge. Leave that to the righteous anger of God. For the Scriptures say, "I will take revenge; I will pay them back," says the Lord. Instead, "If your enemies are hungry, feed them. If they are thirsty, give them something to drink. In doing this, you will heap burning coals of shame on their heads." Don't let evil conquer you, but conquer evil by doing good." Romans 12:14-21

"Jesus told him, "I am the way, the truth, and the life. No one can come to the Father except through me." -John 14:6

Tactical Revival

"Can all your worries add a single moment to your life? And if worry can't accomplish a little thing like that, what's the use of worrying over bigger things?" Luke 12:25-26

"I have told you all this so that you may have peace in me. Here on earth you will have many trials and sorrows. But take heart, because I have overcome the world." -John 16:33

Perilous Healing

"The eyes of then Lord watch over those who do right; his ears are open to their cries for help. But the Lord turns his face against those who do evil; he will erase their memory from the earth. The Lord hears his people when they call to him for help. He rescues them from all their troubles.

The Lord is close to the brokenhearted; he rescues those whose spirits are crushed. The righteous person faces many troubles, but the Lord comes to the rescue each time. For the Lord protects the bones of the righteous; not one of them is broken! Calamity will surely destroy the wicked, and those who hate the righteous will be punished. But the Lord will redeem those who serve him. No one who takes refuge in him will be condemned." -Psalm 34:15-22

"Then Nebuchadnezzar said, "Praise to the God of Shadrach, Meshach, and Abednego! He sent his angel to rescue his servants who trusted in him. They defied the king's command and were willing to die rather than serve or worship any god except their own God." -Daniel 3:28

Some of my other favorite verses:
Ephesians 2:8-9
Philippians 4:13
Romans 8:6
1 Peter 3:10-12

If you have never read the Bible before, and aren't sure where to start, I HIGHLY recommend the New Living Translation Life Application Study Bible. It has been wonderful for really deep diving into the verses and has helped me to understand so much more than I ever have before.

If you are still unsure about taking that step, pray. Ask for God to soften your heart. Ask Him to fill you with the Holy Spirit and help you find your way back to him.

You can always reach out to me if you ever want to talk. jessicaashleyauthor@gmail.com is the best place to reach me.

I pray that these words resonate with you and that God continues to work in your life!

Thank you for reading!

-Jessica

A VETERAN WITH A HEART OF GOLD AND THE WOMAN HE NEVER SAW COMING.

Former Special Forces Operative Bradyn Hunt may have traded a battlefield for his family's ranch in Texas, but that doesn't mean he stopped fighting.

As the founder of Hunt Brother's Search & Rescue, he and his team take on missing persons cases that no one else can solve. They've retrieved people from the very depths of hell-on-earth, which is bound to leave some scars. And he certainly carries his fair share of them.

Kennedy Smith has had many names and lived many different lives. Running from her past, her only goal is to survive long enough to see the next sunrise. Her most recent identity is as a ranch hand in a small North Texas town.

Run by Army veterans, she figures there's no better place to hide than the Hunt family ranch. That is, until she begins to grow attached to the eldest Hunt brother, Bradyn. She should run. After all, not getting attached is rule number one to staying alive. But before she can bring herself to leave, the threat shows up on her doorstep, dragging Bradyn right into the flames alongside her.

Bradyn has saved the lives of hundreds of people, but can he protect Kennedy from the ghosts of her past? Or will her secrets burn everything he's built to the ground?

Scan the QR code above or go to https://geni.us/BravoEB for more information and to pre-order!

If you're looking for a swoony romantic suspense with a protective hero who lives by faith, a team of brothers who follow God, and a woman fighting to survive, then BRAVO is just what you're looking for!

<u>This Christian Romantic Suspense deals with:</u>
-Coping with trauma
-Discovering your worth
-Seeking God in everything
-Healing from your past

The Hunt Brother's Search & Rescue series can be enjoyed in any order, though the suggested reading order is:
Hunt Brothers Search & Rescue: BRAVO
Hunt Brothers Search & Rescue: ECHO
Hunt Brothers Search & Rescue: ROMEO
Hunt Brothers Search & Rescue: DELTA
Hunt Brothers Search & Rescue: TANGO

JESSICA ASHLEY
A COASTAL HOPE NOVELLA
PICTURES of HOPE

About the Author

Jessica Ashley started her career writing spicy romance novels, and had written over sixty before deciding she wanted to use her love of storytelling to help bring people closer to God.

Now, she writes inspirational romance and hopes that each book will draw people closer to seeking His word.

She is an Army veteran, who resides in Texas with her husband and their three children (whom she homeschools).

You can find out more about her and her books by scanning the QR code with your phone's camera, visiting her website: www.authorjessicaashley.com or by joining her Facebook group, Coastal Hope Book Corner.

Scan the QR code below with your phone's camera to connect with her!

Also by Jessica Ashley

<u>Coastal Hope Series</u>

Pages of Promise: Lance Knight

Searching for Peace: Elijah Pierce

Second Chance Serenity: Michael Anderson

Tactical Revival: Jaxson Payne

Perilous Healing: Silas Williamson

COMING SOON:

<u>The Hunt Brothers Search & Rescue</u>

Bravo